EDEN'S
ASHES

THE GARDEN

First Paperback Edition: February 2023

ISBN 978-1-73885-780-7
ISBN 978-1-73885-781-4 (ebook)

I had a dream, it became words, and you were not in it, until I met you.

To my beautiful mother and late father, who I cherish.

CHAPTER

One

I HAD SPENT THE night crying and the flesh under my blue eyes was swollen and sore to the touch. I sat on the wooden floor with my legs up to my chest, my arms wrapped around them, and my head resting on the edge of the sofa.

The floor was made of oak panels, well, not oak, but rather plastic made to resemble the color and texture of oak. More durable, however, when water spilled on them, they warped just like real wood, and the edges curved upward.

The couch was covered in a medium grey fabric and was supported by aluminum legs that I often stubbed my toe on. We all did, and the last time my toe was so black and blue that I had to shuffle my feet when I walked due to the pain. At least I avoided school for a week, I hated school.

Above me, lay my father. He was lying on his side, in almost a fetal position. Sometime in the early morning hours, I covered him fully with the blanket he had been using to keep warm. He was dead.

We lived in a two-bedroom condo on the eleventh floor in a newer building in downtown Toronto. There were windows all the way around, from ceiling to floor, a 'fishbowl' my mother often called it, since everyone could see everything going on inside. Even so, the outside views were spectacular.

We had a balcony that overlooked a courtyard below, a luxury that few condos had, since most were built so closely together. My mother and I often ate dinners on the balcony in the summer months, since my dad habitually worked away from home, sometimes for days at a time.

I didn't enjoy sports and so other than a walk in the nearby park, I would often sit on the balcony and write music on my laptop. I was more interested in music than my schoolwork, and my father was often disappointed by this. So much did his frustration grow, that eventually he gave up looking at my report cards altogether.

I had no idea what time it was. The power was out, and any electrical devices had lost their battery life weeks ago. But it was first light, and I knew that I would have to leave soon.

I didn't want to go. I had never been anywhere without my parents, not even on an overnight trip for school. Something always came up and I just never went.

Only two months ago, my grade six class went to Sudbury, Ontario for a week-long trip, but my father wouldn't allow me. Even though I had never been that far north, I figured I didn't miss much after hearing all the stories. It was all the same kids, causing all the same problems and besides visiting the nickel mine, it didn't sound all that interesting anyways. Then a month later the schools were closed, and I never saw any of my friends again.

Hours earlier my father had whispered that I could not stay in the city and that things would get worse. He didn't have the energy to explain, and I couldn't imagine how. There were no planes, no cars, no visible people, no sounds from neighboring units and the noise that I had learned to tune out since I was born, left me in a blanket of quiet that was unsettling.

In front of me, on the coffee table, was a map of Southern Ontario. A week earlier, he was rummaging through some old filing boxes in the closet. He knew, what I did not. He had the wherewithal to think ahead to this moment, to know where everything was going. In hindsight, he had been displaying the same symptoms that my mother had, coughing, a fever, shortness of breath and then yesterday evening, he was coughing up blood.

My mother lay in the master bedroom and had died days earlier. When she passed, he wouldn't let me see her. He held me back as I tried to enter her room, and put his arms around me tightly, as I cried uncontrollably. He told me that I needed to be brave, to be strong, and he made me promise never to enter the room. I didn't.

It was hard to make the first movement from my lifeless position on the floor, and when I did, the numbness left me, and I felt stiffness in my joints. The grooves in the faux wood floor, left reddish indents in my skin, which I massaged with my hands. I looked at the map. He had drawn a route and told me I needed to follow it exactly.

He had sensed my concern when he told me I had to drive, encouraging me to take it slow. I was eleven, I had never driven in my life. Some other kids' fathers let them take the wheel on side roads or in parking lots – not mine.

I carefully folded the map and put it in the front-left pocket of my jeans. I reached down and felt under the blanket for my father's left arm. His skin was still warm, and his arms were limp, no longer able to provide the security they did days earlier. I unbuckled the leather band from his watch, removed it, and put it in my pocket. It was 8:10 AM.

I walked to my room, which was behind the sofa and a small dining area that we never used except on the rare occasion that we had guests. My door was open, and my bed was still made. I hadn't slept in it in days. The roller blinds were closed letting in only a dim light and I couldn't be bothered to open them. I slid apart the glass closet doors and pulled out my duffle bag.

I got it years earlier. It was part of a give-away campaign from a clothing store my mom had taken me to at the Eaton Centre – a large mall in the downtown core. It made me sad to think of her, how I would never hear her laugh again or spend a quiet evening with her. I wiped a tear from my eye and compartmentalized my thoughts, I needed to stay focused.

I packed some clothes, just like my father had told me, some socks, underwear, pants, shirts, and sweaters. I took my phone and tablet, even though they didn't work. In the hallway outside my door, I took some of the picture frames off the wall and stuffed them in as well.

I dared not open the fridge, anything in there had rotted earlier. I took some cans of food from the cupboard, some tuna, salmon, beans, and some juice boxes – whatever would fit.

I took the keys from the counter and began to walk down the long winding hallway to our front door, passing the washroom on the left and master bedroom on the right. The hallway bent and on the left was the laundry closet and bent again leading to the front door. It was great for reducing the noise from outside the unit, we never heard anyone, but the light did not reach this far, and I could barely see.

I opened the front door, and it was completely dark, lit only dimly by the light under some units' doors – those that did not have the long hallway that we had, often one bedrooms and bachelors.

I left my duffle bag at the door and went back into the kitchen. I opened the utility drawer and found a lighter. Beside the TV there was a large, scented candle. 'Spring Meadow' was written on the side of the brown and beige ceramic container. The candle itself was green and smelled like flowers, or what were supposed to smell like flowers. I lit the candle and put the lighter into my pocket. I walked slowly back to the front door so as not to extinguish the flame, which swayed with each step. I picked up my bag and went out into the hallway.

I was cautious at first, unwilling to close the door behind me. And even though there was nothing stirring in the hallway, I was afraid. I felt like I did on some nights, when I awoke to find my feet dangling over the side of the bed. I would quickly pull them back and under the covers for fear of piranha biting them. Absurd I know, but my fear, nonetheless. I closed our door behind me and began to lock it. Out of habit I suppose since no one would ever come here again I thought, not even me.

As I walked past the neighbor's door, I heard a sound. I put my ear against it, and I could hear crying. It was Joseph. He was my age, and I went to school with him. However, we weren't in any of the same classes, and he played on the basketball team – natural born enemies in terms of the social pecking order. In all the goings on, I never thought about anyone outside our condo until now.

I tapped lightly on the door, still fearful that one of the shadows cast by the candlelight would become someone or something. Footsteps approached the door and stopped. There was a moment of silence, but I could see the light under the door flicker, interrupted by the movement of him inside.

"It's Andrew, from next door," I whispered. I heard the footsteps approach closer.

"Andrew?"

"Yeah, it's me, open up."

A few seconds later, the door opened slightly, and Joseph peered out. Once he saw me, he opened the door wide and embraced me with such a force that I lost my balance. It made me drop the duffle bag and almost extinguished the candle, although the light of the unit filling the hallway, rendered it useless anyways.

We slid down the door frame and sat on the floor, still in an embrace. He began to cry and burrowed himself into me. I tried to reassure him with my pathetic attempt at soothing words, until his crying became a whimper. When his grip loosened, I said the first thing that came to mind.

"I'm leaving and you should come with me." He stared at me a moment. I could see him thinking.

"I can't leave!" he blurted out. His eyes were wide, on the verge of hysteria as he reached back toward the inside of his condo.

"My dad said, it's not safe to stay here. We have to leave," I reasoned holding his face with my hands.

"Where will we go? Where will we go? We can't leave home!" he shouted in panic.

I drew him back toward my chest, trying once again to comfort him. He didn't resist. "I won't leave you, you're safe," I said. He calmed down quickly as I rocked our bodies gently back and forth, the way my mother used to when I awoke from a bad nightmare. If anything were a nightmare, this were it.

I understood what my father had meant. There was no water, and the food would run out. We stay and we die. It's that simple. I had to trust his plan. I had to convince Joseph, but he needed time.

"Come," I said as I tried to take him back into the condo, willing to give it another night.

"No, I don't want to go back inside," he said, his emotion starting to run high again. His reaction reminded me of a cat being thrown into a bathtub as he grabbed my body with his hands.

"Okay," I said calmly, "we don't have to, but we can't stay here." At this he nodded.

"Let me get some things for you," I said, awaiting some acknowledgement before entering his condo and again, he nodded. I looked around the unit. It was a one bedroom, which he shared with his mother. That ruled out getting any of the clothing or belongings from the bedroom. I couldn't handle that.

On an end-table was a picture of him and his mother, which I grabbed and brought back to the door. "We'll take this," I said as I handed it to him. It seemed to please him and again he nodded, this time with a slight smile. He'd be alright I thought.

When the door to his unit closed, we were in the dark again. Lit dimly only by the candle I had put on the floor. Having no power meant the elevators didn't work. We needed to take the stairs.

As we descended, the weight of the duffle bag wore on me. He must have sensed it and took it from my shoulder. He was slightly taller than me, and although just as thin, he had more muscle. His eyes were brown and his hair black, short, and somewhat wavy. We were both sweating, and his hair stuck to his forehead.

Reaching the parking level was bittersweet. The stairs always made me feel claustrophobic and the darkness wasn't helping. The trip downward never seemed to end. Now we would be confronted with an even larger dark space and the small, wired glass window of the exit door offered little reprieve. I opened the door slightly, whispering for Joseph to wait. I was still afraid.

As we exited, the door slammed shut behind us and the sound reverberated through the garage. A sense of alarm jolted through my body causing the hairs on my arms to stand on end. I peered as far as the candlelight allowed, but I could see nothing. If anyone were around, our candlelight would lead them right to us.

We hurried to the car. I pressed the unlock button on the keychain, unlocking the doors and causing the car lights to flash. The lights cast shadows on the surrounding cars and pillars, and I felt a sudden rush of panic. Our walk became a run. Joseph threw the duffle bag in the back and we both got inside and locked the doors. My heart felt as though it were ready to burst through my chest and my breathing was so labored, I had trouble speaking. "We're safe," he said reassuringly as he put his hand on my shoulder. This was so much worse than piranha, I thought.

I felt around the ceiling and turned on the interior light. The candle had already extinguished, and its fragrance turned to a waxy smelling smoke, nothing like the flowers it was supposed to smell like.

We searched for the mechanisms to adjust everything, enough for me to at least see over the steering wheel and reach the pedals.

"I should drive," Joseph joked, "I'm better at it," which was a possible truth since I had never driven in my life.

"Here," I said, removing the map from my pocket.

"What's this?"

"It's where we are heading. You're the navigator."

"I can be that," he laughed, "I'll be the best navigator."

I started the car and put it into gear and the car lunged forward. I pressed the brake suddenly and we both laughed as we were jolted in our seats. We needed levity; It was the first time I laughed in weeks. I turned the wheel and drove toward the garage entrance, which was open.

As we exited, the daylight temporarily blinded us and as our eyes adjusted, we saw a group of boys on the other side of the street. One was striking another boy who lay on the ground with a metal pipe, while another kicked him with his foot.

For a moment, we were transfixed by what we saw unfolding, unable to comprehend the situation. The third assailant drew an axe up over his head to strike the boy on the ground. I could see the all-consuming rage on his face and terror on the other. He brought down the axe upon his victim, splattering blood all over. But he didn't stop, he continued raising and lowering the axe on the boy, dismembering him while he was still alive. I felt weak and faint.

Then one of them saw us and they stopped the bloodshed lowering their weapons to their sides. Their demeanor changed as unexpectedly as a shower on a sunny day.

"Hey," one of the boys called out, smiling, raising his bloody hand to wave as though he had just recognized a friend.

"Go, Andrew go!" Joseph shrieked commandingly.

"We won't hurt you," the boy hollered.

I could feel Joseph shaking me and I could hear him saying my name, but I was fixated on the mutilated body and what had just transpired. I was paralyzed.

CHAPTER

Two

As I started to turn onto the street, their demeanor changed once again. Their faces grew intense with anger, and they ran in our direction with such determination.

One struck the rear driver-side window, smashing the tempered glass, bursting it into small fragments, some of which landed in my lap. He tried to open the rear door, but it was locked, before attempting to climb in.

"Andrew, go!" Joseph yelled again as he struck the boy in the head with his fist. By then the boy with the axe had caught up as well and flung it into our rear window, where it lodged.

Joseph reached his leg over, put his foot on top of mine, and pressed down on the gas pedal. I loosened my grip on the steering wheel, which I still hadn't straightened out from my turn.

As we sped down the street, I could hear the yells of our assailants behind us and what I assumed was the axe falling from the rear window onto the road below.

After a block, I slowed somewhat, turned onto a side street, and pulled over. We were both shaking from the rush of adrenaline, and I rested my head on the steering wheel for a moment.

"They're not behind us," Joseph said. I could see him looking nervously through the passenger side mirror from the corner of my eye. "What was that?" he asked excitedly.

"I don't know," I responded still finding it difficult to breathe. My heart was beating rapidly in my chest, so much I thought it would burst through at any moment. I started to look around at the surrounding buildings and alleyways for any sign of movement, worried that someone else would descend upon us, but there was no one.

"We should drive," he said.

"Just give me a minute," I responded, putting my head down.

"Do you want me to drive?"

I shook my head.

"We need to get out of here Andrew," he said imploringly, while still looking around.

I nodded. I hadn't even put the vehicle into park realizing that my foot was still pressed hard against the brake pedal. I softened its hold and began to drive slowly down the street.

The streets were deserted and if it weren't for what just happened, it wouldn't be hard to believe were we the only two people left. I found myself braking to traffic lights that were all without power and for which there was no traffic.

Joseph was disengaged and stared out the window. He then turned toward the door and started to sob.

I didn't want to stop, but I had to. I couldn't focus on both him and driving. I put my hand on his shoulder.

"Are you okay?" I asked him. But he never replied. I gave him a few minutes and found myself being both attentive to him and our surroundings. "We're going somewhere safe," I said to him comfortingly. His whimpers lessened.

"How do you know that?"

"Because I trust my dad and I know he wouldn't tell me to do this if he didn't think it were safe."

Joseph nodded and turned to look at me.

"I know how to get to the highway," I said, "but not after that. Why don't you focus on following the map, and I'll keep a look out as I drive?"

He nodded again and unfolded the map in his lap. I don't think either of us had really used one. We were so used to our phones, and it took him some time to figure out where we were before he could start directing me.

The focus of driving and reading the map distracted both of us somewhat. My family had driven this route many times, but I had never paid much attention. Joseph wanted me to drive faster, but I mostly ignored him since my father had told me to take my time. I wasn't sure whether this was because he wanted to get out of the city, an impossibility of sorts since its boundaries never seemed to end, or whether he wanted some excitement. After what we had just experienced, I chose to believe the former.

"Do we have any food?" he asked and when I nodded my head toward the back, he reached over into the duffle bag. He was thinking about food, so I knew he was feeling better. "Are you hungry or thirsty?"

"I'm starved," I responded. I hadn't eaten anything since yesterday.

"Everything's canned," he said. I glanced at him with an apologetic look on my face. He then opened one of the juice boxes and handed it to me, while he took another.

It was 12:25 PM already. As we drove along the highway, we mostly stayed quiet, keeping an eye out. There were some parked cars on the highway, abandoned, perhaps out of gas from those who tried to escape. But to where? There was no escaping. The virus had affected everyone.

We passed places that we recognized, shopping centers, a movie theatre, restaurants, all closed, all abandoned and the stark reality set in that we would never see these places again.

After about another hour of highway driving, we reached my sister's house in Bolton, where I pulled into the driveway.

The house was a bungalow made of a light beige brick and had a red shingled roof. The large front yard, characteristic of older homes, was landscaped with lots of flowers, lilac bushes, and a cedar tree. The lawn had been neglected. It had grown in and was speckled with yellow dandelions.

I had two sisters, who both lived in the house, one on the main level with my eldest niece and her brother, and the other in the basement with her three daughters.

I could see some of them watching from the front living room window and so I waved, although I wasn't sure if they could see me through the windshield or even knew it were me driving.

It had been months since I'd last seen them. They would seldom visit us in the city, and my parents and I would mostly make the drive. I didn't mind. There weren't many parks in the downtown core, and I enjoyed the greenery of the burbs. Besides, our condo was too small to hold so many visitors.

"Who are they?" Joseph asked.

"My nieces and nephews."

"You have nieces and nephews? You're like, my age." I could feel my face flush with embarrassment.

"I know, everyone says that, but my dad remarried, and my parents had me when they were older." I could tell he was still confused. Most were. I hated telling people. The reaction was always the same. Most kids believed that you had to be older to be an uncle, when it was simply a matter of relation.

I put the vehicle into park and turned off the engine. The front door of the house opened, and my eldest niece Mia peered out the storm door. "You ready?" he asked. I nodded.

As we exited the car, however, I realized that I wasn't ready. I suddenly felt exposed, no longer protected by the metal confines of the car that shielded us earlier, or the long uninterrupted highway with its tall noise barriers. In the subdivision, I felt unsafe, the weight of people from the surrounding houses watching us.

I neglected surveying the damage to the car and hurried up the concrete steps to the front door. Joseph lagged. I put my finger to my mouth, instructing those inside to be quiet.

I went to the window, which was covered by horizontal blinds, and I began to draw them closed. I looked out into the sub-division, at the windows of the other houses. In some, I could see movement and in others, indiscernible faces, staring back. I wondered if they could see me through the blinds, but they had seen us arrive, so it didn't matter.

I took my father's watch from my pocket. It was now two in the afternoon. We could hurry and leave, but we'd be pushing it since we had a long drive ahead of us. I then became aware of everyone around me, and the sad look on their faces. Joseph had already introduced himself, but I had forgone the usual salutations.

"What's wrong Andrew?" Joseph asked.

"There are people in the houses," I whispered.

"But we're safe, we're inside," he said.

I realized I had caused concern among the younger of them. I nodded and tried to force a smile, but I'm sure it came across as ingenuine.

I wasn't so sure that we were safe. The front-door was hardly protection from anyone who really wanted to get in. I had felt safer in the condo. There was only one main door, which could be barricaded, and no one could scale the glass walls of the building to reach us.

I sat on the floor under the windowsill. Chloe crossed the room and sat beside me resting her head on my arm, which I put around her. She was only five and was rather quiet and shy for her age, but I adored her.

"Where is grandma and grandpa?" her sister Madison asked. I shook my head. "That means they're dead, doesn't it?" she yelled, "they're all dead!" I motioned with my other arm for her to come and sit beside me, but she retreated to the kitchen sulking and Mia went after her. At this Chloe began to cry and I picked her up and went to stand in the doorway between the kitchen and living room.

"Grandpa told me to come here and take you to a place he drew on a map," I said.

"Which place?" Violet asked.

Joseph pulled out the map from his pocked and laid it on the coffee table, while everyone crowded around.

"Here," Joseph pointed after tracing the next leg of our journey.

"Crawford Lake?" Mia asked, "what's at Crawford Lake?"

"Not exactly," I responded pointing to a crude drawing on the side of the map, "it's some place a little south of there."

"But what's there?" Mia asked again.

"I don't know. Some place he felt would be safe for us to go."

They all looked at the map, although I am sure even the older of us could barely understand it. "Tonight, we can pack and early tomorrow we can awaken and leave," I said.

This seemed to give most a newly found purpose, although not everyone was content with the decision. Madison began to cry again, triggering Chloe. They missed their parents. Madison and Chloe were one of my brother's kids, but they shouldn't have been here.

"How did they get here?" I asked Mia.

"Their dad dropped them off and he never came back," she replied. I crouched down and hugged both Madison and Chloe until their crying abated once again.

Violet and Bella focused on packing what was in the kitchen while most of the others focused on packing up clothes from two of the bedrooms. I figured the reason they were avoiding the other bedroom was because my sister and her husband were probably in there.

"How are we all going to fit in one car?" Joseph asked.

"We aren't. We're going to take both cars," I responded decisively. "Hopefully, the other car has gas."

"Who's going to drive the other?"

"Mia."

"I could drive the other."

"You? You're my navigator!" I responded with a grin.

"I can drive," Daniel blurted out.

"You're *nine*," I responded dismissingly.

"Yeah, well she's only one year older," he retorted.

"It shows," I said with a chuckle. "Mia drives. Me, Joseph, Bella, Luna, and Violet, in one car, Mia, Daniel, Madison, and Chloe, in the other."

I could tell that he wasn't pleased with this, but I was tired and all I cared about right now was making it through the rest of the journey. The last thing we needed was for half of us to meet some fiery demise because an immature nine-year old can't tell the difference between a real car and the one he plays in Grand Theft Auto. I wasn't even sure how he was able to survive without his gaming console. Every time I visited, he was glued to it, and barely spoke a comprehensible sentence. Mia was mature for her age, responsible.

"What about Ava and Hannah?" Mia asked.

"Who are they?" Joseph asked.

"My other brother's kids."

"They live in Shelburne," Mia added.

"You have a big family," Joseph said.

"From my dad's first marriage," I responded. "Shelburne isn't on the map," I said.

"Did grandpa say anything about them?" Violet asked.

I shook my head. He never said anything about Madison and Chloe either, but here they were. Until arriving here, the thought never crossed my mind. I had been too focused on following directions to think.

"We have to get to Crawford Lake," I said.

"But they must be scared," Mia replied.

I walked away from the coffee table for a moment and stared out the blinds again. "Shelburne is at least an hour from here, and then we'd have to drive further to get to Crawford Lake. We won't have enough gas. We could get them afterwards though."

But upon saying that I wasn't even sure that was a good idea because then we'd be separated. My dad must have known this, and I was now perplexed as to why he never explicitly drew this on the map. Was it simply because the map didn't show Shelburne? But then he didn't mention it either. "Let me think," I said and then realized I had nowhere else to really go except the Kitchen and Living room.

"We need to go downstairs and get the other belongings and there's more food down there," I said after a few minutes, trying to change the subject and find an excuse to get away from everyone. I needed to take my mind off the problem for a while.

I looked at the door to the basement and realized that there was another problem.

"Do you know where *they* are at?" I asked Mia, in reference to my other sister and her husband. She understood what I meant and shook her head. I looked at Violet and Bella who was busy packing some of the canned food, and I didn't want to bring it up.

Joseph and I opened the door that led to the basement and began descending the steep stairs. I had always hated these stairs for fear that I would fall. A few years ago, during a visit, Daniel had fallen. It sounded as though he hit every step, and after a moment of silence at the bottom, he began to cry. The railing was shaky and just like everyone else would do, I put my hand on the wall instead, following the trail of grime that had built up over the years.

The dank smell of the basement increased with each step. The dehumidifier obviously wasn't running, and a new smell permeated the air – the smell of death. My stomach churned loudly, and I began shaking a bit.

"You alright?" Joseph asked as I stopped in place about halfway down.

"Yeah," I said unsurely, nodding. In actuality, I wasn't okay, and I wasn't looking forward to the possibility of seeing the bodies of my other sister and her husband.

The door to the basement apartment was closed and I fumbled to find the handle in the darkness. It would lead into an open concept kitchen and living room, a necessity considering that the small windows of the basement didn't allow much natural light to enter. I opened the door slowly, not knowing whether their bodies would be on the other side and a slight relief dawned on me when I saw they were not.

I led Joseph into the kitchen and opened the pantry cupboard, which was about the size of a refrigerator. We found some bags and began putting the food into them. "I've got this," he said.

I walked toward the back of the apartment, where there were two bedrooms and a washroom. The doors to both bedrooms were closed. I slowly opened the door of the kid's bedroom, and a subtle amount of light entered the room revealing the shapes of the dresser and bunk beds. And on one of them lay my brother-in-law. I was so overcome by the stench that I collapsed on my hands and knees and began to vomit the stomach acid and apple juice that was inside. It burned my throat. My heart raced and I felt a hot sweat come over me as I fumbled for the handle to close the door.

Joseph came running and pulled me up to a sitting position before dragging me through to the living room where we sat on the floor near the sofa.

"Are you guys okay?" Mia hollered from the top of the stairs. I realized that sound carried easily through the wooden floors and that we had left the apartment door open.

"Yeah," Joseph hollered back. He grabbed a juice box from the kitchen and handed it to me to sip on. "Drink slowly," he said. Clothes be damned, I thought. There would be enough upstairs.

After a few minutes, I assured him that I was alright, and he went back to packing the food from the pantry into bags. I left him to task and looked around the room.

My sister relished photography, and she had made a heart shape on the wall using various picture frame sizes with the word "LOVE" in the center. I always detested such décor; they had become ordinary and boring, a staple of most homes. However, this was different. I took a few of the pictures from the wall, and this left the heart broken. The irony, I thought, since it was how I felt. I had lost my mom, dad, both sisters, and probably both brothers.

I added them to one of the bags in the kitchen and finished helping him pack.

We brought the bags upstairs and combined with what everyone else had packed, we amassed enough bags to fit on top of the kitchen table and the surrounding floor.

"This is too much," Mia said.

"We need the food," Joseph said, to which we all simply nodded. "Let's go through the clothing and get rid of anything that we don't really need."

This was an emotional exercise as everyone had something they really wanted. A certain t-shirt or dress, a favorite teddy bear or doll. Sometimes I found myself wanting to slyly take something from the pile and throw it aside, but I didn't. I let them decide and eventually we cut the number of items down by a third.

"It still seems like a lot," Mia said again.

"I think we can make it work," I said.

"And when we go to Shelburne?" she asked, bringing up the topic again.

"I don't know about that yet," I said.

"They'll die," Violet interrupted.

Usually she was happy and lighthearted, never seemingly sad, but those words were it. The gas be damned, the obstacles be damned, I nodded my head. "Okay, we will go."

That night, I found myself sitting within the living room in the pink recliner. It always seemed out of place amongst the beige walls and brown furniture. I had turned it to face out the window and sat with my legs tucked under me. I peered through the small string holes of the closed blinds.

The surrounding neighborhood was quiet. There was no movement. The shapes that stood in the windows of the houses across the street earlier, had disappeared into the blackness. Perhaps they were doing the same thing I thought, staring back at us, trying to pierce the darkness to see into our windows.

There was little movement inside the living room either. The cries and whimpers of the evening had given way, first to fatigue, and then sleep, only interrupted by the slight snoring of a few and the sudden jerks of others. Nightmares I thought.

I noticed Mia's eyes were open and staring at me. "Why don't you sleep?" she whispered, "you must be exhausted." I was, but after seeing what we had in the morning, I had to keep us safe. I hadn't shared that. I didn't want anyone to be afraid. There was enough to be afraid of already.

"Did you know them?" I whispered back.

"Who?" she responded.

"The kids across the street."

"Yes, but we weren't friends, they bullied Daniel." I simply nodded and resumed my surveillance.

The night began rather uneventful. I heard a metal garbage can somewhere in the distance being knocked over, probably Racoons I reasoned fearing worse, but other than that, nothing but dead silence.

Then I heard it, the sound a stone makes when scraped underfoot on pavement. I looked at Mia who was once again sleeping. I listened intently and tried peering out the blinds, but I could see no one. Then the unmistakable sound of weight on the uneven concrete steps. Could it be? Someone was at our front door.

CHAPTER

Three

I LEFT MY PLACE in the chair and walked swiftly but stealthily to the front door and listened. The slight rattle of the door handle and slow squeak of metal as it turned, drew my glance downward. Whoever it was, they were trying to get in!

I panicked and checked that the deadbolt was still locked – it was. The door budged as they pushed against it, enough to startle me and reawaken Mia.

I signaled for her to be quiet and then pointed to Joseph in rapid succession. "Wake him," I whispered as authoritatively as I could without raising my voice. The stranger pushed the door again, recapturing my attention, before retreating down the concrete steps. Had they heard me? They couldn't have I thought. That's when I turned my attention to the back of the house.

Mia, Daniel, and Joseph were up. "There's someone trying to get in," I whispered while walking quickly to the kitchen. Daniel ran into his room and produced a baseball bat. Fitting, I thought.

I drew the window blinds in the kitchen and then turned my focus to the back door. It was old and, fearing it would not hold, I sat with my back against it. I waved for Joseph to come and do the same and I motioned for Mia and Daniel to go back into the living room so they wouldn't be seen.

We waited and sure enough moments later, I heard the slow approach of the strangers steps up the deck stairs. They were trying to be quiet, but the porch was as old as the house, and the boards creaked. They paused outside the door, and I wondered if they were trying to look through the glass pane at the top. I drew my legs up to my knees and motioned Joseph with my hand to do the same, so they wouldn't see them.

They tried the handle, which I reached up to hold in place. The door shifted as they tried to open it. More so than the front door, but it held. There was a long pause and the prowler left once again.

I gazed out the kitchen blinds and watched as the shadowy figure crept across the lawn, stopping to look into the basement windows. They were too narrow for someone to crawl through, although perhaps not for a child I thought. I watched for a moment, as they continued walking around to the front of the house.

I whispered to Joseph to stay and watch the back while I took the bat and went into the living room. I looked out the front window to see if I could catch another glimpse of them, but there was no sign.

I stood, worried, listening, uncertain about where this person may try next. I went from one room to another looking out the windows, but I could see no one.

As the night drew on, there were no further signs of the stranger. I encouraged the others to go back to sleep, that I would continue to keep watch, me with a baseball bat, as I sat perched back in the pink chair.

Maybe it was someone searching for food, I reasoned. There was little I took from the condo and while there was a lot that we had gathered, it would hardly last us any real amount of time. Would we have to do the same, scour for food? I had no idea where my dad was directing us, or what would even be there. He had kept his instructions so succinct. Or maybe it was someone looking for trouble, someone who had seen us arrive. But it didn't appear so. They came, they tried to enter, they couldn't, they left. Surely anyone really wanting to enter could have.

When the morning light came, it shone into the windows of the houses across the street, making their interiors visible, but there was no one in sight. The shadows that lurked within them yesterday had disappeared. The streets were empty and there was no trace of the stranger who visited us through the night.

Slowly, tired bodies began to rise from the floor, and sit half-awake, perched lazily on the edges of sofas and in various corners around the room. The streaming shows, phones, social media, all of which we obsessed over, were things of mornings past. Now we had little to occupy our minds.

Violet was one of the first up along with Joseph, and I left my post hesitantly to join them both in the kitchen.

"We've run out of bread," she announced looking through the bags of food that were packed on the kitchen table. She was unaware of what had happened through the night, and I figured it was best to keep it that way. At least she wouldn't hear it from me. I poked through the bags and pulled out a box of vegetable crackers and digestifs.

"We can eat these," I said, and then pulled out a half-empty jar of strawberry jam, "and this."

"You look tired," Joseph whispered to me as Violet began to prepare plates of jam covered crackers. "Did you sleep at all?" I shook my head.

"I'll be okay," I responded as I walked back to the recliner and resumed my surveillance. I don't think he believed me; I don't think I even believed myself.

The house was built several decades ago and no one in the surrounding neighborhood had bothered to erect new fences. The original green chain-link fence that the builder had installed stood only half-height and made the sightlines clear. Leaving through the back would possibly alert more to our presence and so I once again left through the front door.

I hurried to my sister's car, worried that last night's stranger might still be nearby. I unlocked it, put the key in the ignition, and checked the gas gauge.

It was half-full, about the same as my car. I hoped it would be enough to get us to Crawford Lake, but I wasn't sure. What I was sure of, was that it wouldn't be enough to take us the full journey to Shelburne and then to Crawford Lake.

I exited the car and surveyed the area. There was no sign of the stranger. The hedge beside the driveway towered high above me and provided some privacy. I peered through its branches and the street beyond was barren.

I began carrying loads from the house to the cars, one bag at a time. We should have done this last night, I thought. Stranger or no stranger, the darkness would have provided us cover. Now anyone watching would see that we were getting ready to leave and that could be a problem.

And I was right. Only a few moments later a girl and boy emerged from the house across the street.

At first, I was taken aback. After yesterday's attack, I found myself gauging their emotion wondering if they were a threat. I looked at Joseph who had been handing me the bags from the front door. He began to step out, but I motioned him with a subtle wave to stay put.

The couple stared back at me. Maybe they would go back inside, I thought, but then they began to walk across their yard toward me. They walked slowly, cautiously. Their faces wore the sorrow that all of us were feeling, and the boy had been visibly crying.

"Stay there," I commanded when they were nearing the end of our driveway. I could hear the uneasiness in my own voice. The two stopped.

"Are you leaving? Can you take us with you?" the girl blurted out.

Desperation. Perhaps I never felt that because my father had given me a plan. I never had time to think about what I would do, I hadn't even slept. I was still following his directions. I struggled to find the words to explain what I already knew we couldn't do. Or what I wouldn't do.

We didn't have the room and certainly I wouldn't want someone who tormented Daniel along for the ride. And while I didn't know what awaited us, what I did know is that our strength as a group would depend on it. Taking them wouldn't be like taking Joseph. No, that was different. He wasn't someone entirely unknown to me, and while we hadn't been friends in school, he wasn't like the other athletic boys. Something was different. He had a humility about him.

The boy was holding the girl's hand and I sensed him trying to pull away from her, but she grasped tighter. I blurted out my thoughts as firm and emotionless as I could, "We can't take the two of you with us," I said, "we don't have room."

The boy began to cry. I looked at the surrounding houses, fearful that his crying would alert more to our presence. He pulled harder at her hand, and she grasped even tighter. This confused me. When he managed to escape her grasp, he came running and grabbed onto my leg.

The girl crouched down, "Nathan, come here now," she said gently, almost soothingly, and for a moment she reminded me of my mother.

The boy glanced at her and ceased his crying as though captivated by her. I thought he would release his hold and return to her, but he turned once again and buried his head into me, holding on tighter than ever, almost knocking me from my feet.

Her demeanor changed as she stood and began to walk toward me and the child angrily. "Stay there," I demanded putting out my hand. I felt vulnerable with my uneasy footing. She grabbed the boy and forcefully pulled him off me, causing me to fall to the ground.

"Hey!" Joseph yelled, leaving his place on the steps, and swiftly walking toward us. I held him back with my hands. The boy continued crying and reaching back toward me, fighting the girl as she dragged him back into the home across the street. I could hear the boy crying, her yelling, and then silence.

"Are you okay?" Joseph asked.

"Yeah, yeah," I said nodding my head, wiping the dirt from the back of my pants.

"That was weird," he said.

I nodded. "We'd better get this finished."

We resumed hastily packing the cars. I wanted to leave, we had overextended our stay and I was worried the entire episode would draw more attention. There were other kids in the sub-division. Lots of them. I remembered coming to the house one Halloween, a couple of years earlier, and at least a hundred kids visited. The fact that they weren't lined up now was nothing short of a miracle.

Had I made the right decision? I felt bad, especially for the boy. My throat tingled, the way I did when I ate popping candy. We couldn't take him though, not without taking her.

I was just finishing up when the boy emerged again from the house screaming and running toward us. His face had streams of blood on it and behind him, the girl exited running after him. I was aghast with horror and paralyzed.

I stood still, unsure of what was unfolding. "Andrew," Joseph yelled startling me as he grabbed my hand and pulled me toward the house. "Wait," I pleaded, as the others wanted me to close the door. I stood in the frame, reaching for the boy's hand, beckoning for him to run faster. But it was too late. She caught up to him and subdued him, like a hawk catching a mouse, and dragged him back to their house once again. I felt eviscerated. There was nothing I could do.

Joseph moved me inside and locked the door. I stood, staring at the now solid surface. "We have to leave, now," he said, "everyone, come on, we're leaving."

"What's happening out there?" Mia asked. I simply shook my head, unsure of what to make of it all. Joseph continued to gather everyone, and the few things left.

Then, there was a knock on the door. It was the girl. She was back again. "It's only *me* now, can you take me with you?" she asked weeping. Her voice now gentle and faint, but ingenuine.

I looked at the others puzzled. What did she mean? Joseph shook his head; he must have thought I would open the door.

"What about the boy?" I asked. I waited intently for her to respond as all manner of thoughts streamed through my head. What had happened to him? Why was he covered in blood?

She then let out a chilling laugh, "take me with you."

"We can't," I said.

"But you said, you can't take two of us, now there's only one," she responded. My skin went icy cold, and goosebumps covered my arms. Had she killed him? "Take me with you," she said again, this time louder and angrily. I stepped back momentarily from the door. She repeated the phrase again, beginning an unrelenting pounding on the door screaming all sorts of obscenities and incomprehensible utterances.

I held the door with my body, fearful that she would burst through. Although she would be outnumbered, she was hysterical.

"What do we do?" I asked holding the door. Daniel came and held it with me.

"She's lost her mind," Joseph said. And after a few minutes, it seemed as though it had stopped, until a rock hurled through the living room window breaking the first pane of glass.

"Everyone, get to the back," I yelled covering my head to shield myself from it.

I could hear her grunt with effort as she threw another rock, breaking the second pane of glass. She then tried to reach the lock from the broken window. I fought with her arm, trying to keep it from the door, but she was persistent and surprisingly strong.

Then Daniel approached and hit her arm with his baseball bat, startling me. I could hear what sounded like a bone snap and she let out a single scowl. The crying stopped; the yelling stopped. I could hear her descend once again down the steps and I watched her through the broken window as she stomped back toward her house.

All of us were shaken by the ordeal. Many of the younger kids were crying. We couldn't stay, not with the commotion that took place and with the windows smashed out the way they were. Certainly now, there would be others who might be curious or bold enough to come around. And while the door still provided me a sense of security, it was imagined. I knew that. Anyone could easily enter now, and we would have little recourse. We'd have no place to go.

The three kids in Toronto could have easily subdued us if Joseph hadn't awaked me from my stupor. I didn't know what to do, but at the same time I felt we had to leave immediately. Everyone else seemed pre-occupied, consoling each other, and I stared around at their faces. The onus was on me to direct our next move, and I felt physically sickened by it.

I didn't want to go outside again. I wanted to find a corner, away from everyone and everything, huddle in it, and cry. I wanted my mother back. I wanted to hear her voice, be cuddled in her arms, wrapped in a blanket watching a Saturday night movie. But instead, I was here, standing beside a door with glass around my feet, realizing the impossibility of that normal ever being a part of my life again. That all of us, here now, we're all that we had.

"Okay," I said, mustering up whatever of the little strength I had. I was certain my voice broke a little as everyone looked in my direction. "We're leaving. Right now."

After a few minutes we were all in both cars driving down the street of the sub-division. We never saw the girl or boy again. My adrenaline was still rushing, and it wasn't until thirty minutes or so before my heart reached a normal pace. The driving, more so the focus on driving, helped. The others were still talking about what had happened, replaying the event over, but I tuned them out.

When we reached the town limits, I stopped at a gas station. I figured that it would be safe – it was surrounding by nothing but fields. The windows of the station were smashed out and most of the place ransacked. The smell of rotting goods from the fridges saturated the air and flies were in abundance. I looked through the maps on display, which were still fully stocked, and found one for Shelburne. I then grabbed a basket and began filling it with any foodstuffs that remained, which weren't much, mostly those things no one cared for, like canned ham and beef jerky. I didn't care though; anything was better than nothing.

The drive to Shelburne was difficult to say the least. After about thirty minutes, I began to nod off and Joseph took over. Violet sat in the passenger seat to help with the map, and I climbed into the very back and nestled myself amongst the softer of the garbage bags. I was too tired or exhausted to cry, but I wanted to and would have if I didn't succumb to sleep. I slept for about an hour, and well at that, before I was awakened once again. Bella was shaking me, "Andrew, we're here."

My brother's house was atypical for a suburban home. Unlike the others, it didn't face the street and was surrounded by tall pine trees. I pulled into his driveway and drove into his large front yard, which resembled more of a small field. Mia followed.

The house was quiet, and no one came to the door to greet us when I knocked. I peered into the windows, but the inside was too dark to see – the trees blocking out most of the sunlight.

I tried the door, but it was locked. I knocked. Nothing. "Ava? Hannah?" I spoke closely to the door, but no one answered. I listened intently for any noise, but all was quiet.

I looked back at the cars, where some of the kids had begun to exit. "Can you get them back inside?" I asked Mia waving my hand in the direction of the car. They needed to stretch, but I was still cognizant of the ordeal we had gone through only hours ago. I tried knocking again, but there was nothing.

"Are they not at home?" Joseph asked.

"It's possible," I said staring at the house expecting them to emerge at any moment. Even the sound of the car should have been enough to make them aware of our presence.

I picked up a rock and, with little thought, threw it into the window next to the door. The sound alarmed everyone. It probably wasn't the smartest thing to do and a part of me wanted to head back to the safety of the car. It wasn't a clean break and large fragments of glass remained in the frame, some half the height of me. I found a stick from the nearby tree line and began pushing the slabs of glass inside, each one shattering as it fell.

I would have imagined that if anyone were home, the noise alone would have been enough to warrant attention, but there was nothing.

"Ava? Hannah?" I called out again through the now open window, but my calls went unheeded.

I needed to get inside but doing so would be difficult. Not only would I need to climb up and through the window, but a lot of broken glass now lay on the other side.

I emptied a backpack from the car and slung it over the window ledge. Joseph helped lift me up and I must have said careful at least a dozen times, for fear that I would fall over and into the glass laying on the floor. When I got inside, I nervously glanced around at the quiet interior and opened the front door. Joseph remained in the entrance to keep an eye out.

"Ava? Hannah?" I repeated. They weren't in the living room in which I was standing or in the adjacent kitchen. Everything looked in its place and orderly. I slowly walked back toward the bedrooms. "Ava? Hannah" I spoke softly, "it's me, Andrew." There was no response.

When I reached their bedroom door, I opened it slowly and walked up to their bed, where they were sleeping. "Ava? Hannah?" I whispered. I went to shake them, but they were cold and stiff. They were dead.

CHAPTER
Four

I STRUGGLED TO GASP for air and ran out the door of the bedroom, closing it behind me. I collapsed with my back against it and cupped my face with my hands as I started to cry.

"Andrew?" Joseph hollered as he ran into the house and down the hall toward where I sat, sliding onto his knees next to me.

"They're dead," I cried out, "they're all dead!" He held me in his arms the same way I had done a day earlier.

"Is everything alright?" Mia called from the door.

"Stay there, we're coming," Joseph hollered back. But we never, we just sat and cried.

After a while, he looked at my face. His eyes showed such concern. Unexpectedly, he took his sleeve and wiped the dried tears from my tired eyes and face. I nodded to indicate I was alright. He stood up and reached down for my hand to help me up and led me outside with his arm around my shoulder. We emerged from the front door and stood on the steps, and I took some deep breaths. All their eyes were on me. I didn't have to say anything, they all understood and cried.

But I had no more tears. Everyone was dead and I was spent. I glanced at my father's watch; it was now two o'clock. I steadfastly checked the gas in the car. It was now less than a quarter of a tank.

"We have to get out of here," I said, "we can't stay here."

Joseph once again tried to comfort me. "You're not ready Andrew," he said quietly, but I spurned his attempts to soothe me. He may have been right, but the last thing I wanted was to stay in another sub-division for the night. We should have never come, I thought.

"I'm okay," I said gently pushing past him and walking back into the house to open the garage.

"We'll they're not," he continued.

"I'll do everything, they can relax," I responded dismissively.

I started rummaging through the various boxes and tool chests, which my brother had lots of. They were covered with oil and layers of dust, which stuck to them and turned them shades paler than their original colors. He didn't work, which is probably why they looked the way they did. My mother would always give him money and my dad, whilst never saying anything in the presence of my brother, would make his feelings known on the way home. My parents rarely argued, but on this matter they did, like clockwork. It sucked any joy out of our visits. It had been so long since our last visit, I struggled to remember what it was like and that frustrated me even further.

"What are you looking for?" Mia asked, as I mumbled to myself.

"A syphon, a hose, he has to have one somewhere here... he was always tinkering with cars, there has to be one," I said annoyed by all the excess waste.

At that, Joseph and Mia began to help and a few minutes later, Mia produced one from under a shelf.

I opened the gas cover of my brother's truck. "We need something to put it in," I said, taking the syphon from Mia and putting it in the tank. Moments later Joseph found a Jerry Can.

I syphoned the gas until the can was full. It smelled. I then waited for Joseph to pour it into our car and then did the same again for the other. I repeated the process in tandem, trying to get equal amounts into both cars.

"Hey Mia, can you check it?" I asked before tossing her my keys.

"It's half-full," she said, her voice muffled by the interior of the car.

I pulled my father's watch from my pocket. First wiping my hands on my shirt so it wouldn't get covered in oil and gas residue.

"We leave now," I said getting back into the car.

"Andrew, the kids are hungry," Mia said coming around to the window with Joseph by her side. I lowered it and put my hands and head on the steering wheel. I wanted to cry again, but I couldn't.

"Not now, please. I don't want to stay here any longer," I replied frustratingly.

"Maybe we could stop a little way down the road and take out some food?" Joseph said. I nodded.

Mia and Joseph look at each other, "I'm okay," I said loudly, reassuring them again, even though it was so far from the truth.

We shouldn't have come, I thought again. We lost of hours of time, and I could have led the others in harm's way. I never wanted to come, but I let my emotions get in the way. I had no idea how my father knew, but he would have drawn it or mentioned it if he knew they were alive. Certainly, he wouldn't have wanted us to leave them behind. Ava and Hannah, left to fend for themselves. Impossible.

The focus on driving helped once again take my mind off it all.

After two hours of driving, we neared Crawford Lake, a conservation area north of Burlington, a city that I had only ever driven through a few times with my parents. The car was getting low on gas, and I was sure that the weight of us all crammed into the vehicle wasn't helping.

"There's the sign, on the left," Joseph said pointing as we drove south on Guelph Line. The wooden sign sat almost obscured by deciduous trees. 'Crawford Lake' was written on it vertically in green letters.

My parents and I had been to Crawford Lake many times before and while I remembered the sign, I guess I was always too preoccupied to really take notice of it.

"Not that entrance though," he said as I slowed and began to turn to the left. "Sorry, it's a little further down," he said looking ahead briefly while continuing to focus on the markings my father had made on the map.

The road near the sign led to a pay booth, visitors center and large parking lots. There was also an Iroquoian village, well, a reconstruction of what one may have looked like. It was based on archeologists finding corn at the bottom of Crawford Lake, ever preserved in the meromictic water. Although I had been to it a few times, I was more interested in the nature of the surrounding area.

We continued to drive, and on the left, the forest gave way to a large swamp. The water almost reached the surface of the road, and I was sure that possibly weeks earlier, with the spring rain, it would have covered the road completely. It had been a wet spring. Tall trees, footed by reeds, surrounded the water, some of them fallen, stretching out from the shores. The water was not very deep though, and the sunlight illuminated the sandy bottom.

"There! There it is!" Joseph exclaimed, distracting me from my thoughts. To the left was a small road, at an angle that was almost a full turn back to the north. The pavement gave way to a dirt road no wider than a single car.

"Are they following us?" I asked Joseph since it was too hard for me to see through the rear-view mirror. I could see him peering in the side mirrors, trying to catch a glimpse before answering. I had asked him so many times during the drive, that I was surprised he wasn't visibly bothered by it.

The road twisted and curved through the forest, whose floor was covered with large boulders, and a vibrant green moss. The sun shined in the clear blue sky, blocked only by tree branches, whose shadows moved on the car windshield as we drove.

"Stop here," Joseph said as we approached a side road on the left. The road was recently covered with fresh earth and seemed so out of place against the worn road we were travelling on. "We should turn here," he said looking at the map. The single-lane road opened into a small lot.

"Is this it?" I asked.

"It has to be," Joseph said concentratedly, trying to confirm his answer by looking at the map.

I put the vehicle into park and Mia pulled up her vehicle beside us. "Stay here," I said exiting, loudly enough that the occupants of the other car could hear me. But Joseph came out soon after and ran around the front to catch up. I motioned the others to stay put using my hand. They seemed to understand although they began clamoring into the now vacant front seats.

The lot was surrounded by forest and in front of us was the rockface of a cliff that stood at least twenty feet tall. On top of the cliff were more trees. Roots hung over the rockface, exposed, and intertwined with the rock itself. Small streams of water trinkled their way through the rock, giving life to moss, and formed puddles on the ground.

"What's that?" Joseph asked pointing. A shallow cave lay sunken within the face and inside its darkness was a faint, green glow.

I walked forward cautiously. As we approached the cave, a metal door became visible through the darkness. It was painted a dull grey, almost the same color as the surrounding rock, making it difficult to see. Beside the door was a numeric pad, embedded within the rock, that had a bright green display.

"There's power!" Joseph exclaimed almost jumping up and down with excitement, "were they not affected out here?" I envied his energy. I wasn't sure where he got it from, but I could use even an ounce of it.

"We never saw anyone all the way here," I said. I glanced around to see if anyone was watching us, but it was only my anxiety getting the better of me.

"Should we knock?" Joseph asked and before I could answer, he did.

"I doubt anyone is here." My dad never mentioned it at all, and the lot was empty. I could tell that Joseph was analyzing the expression on my face and I wondered what he was thinking. "So, how do we get in?" I said diverting his glare. As if he would have the answer any more than I would. He appeared in thought.

"Hold on a second," Joseph said running back to the passenger side of the car, where he produced the map. He unfolded the map fully and, on the top, right corner, were four numbers. "This must be it," he said entering the numbers, '1102'.

"That's just my condo number," I said to him flatly, "you live right beside me, I doubt..." and a second later, the metal door slid open.

In front of me stood a large, round, glass terrarium. It emerged from below the floor and extended to the top of the ceiling. It was brightly lit, although the light barely penetrated the surrounding darkness. The interior was obscured by thick mist and vegetation. There was no one here it seemed, and the only other light was from the daylight pouring in from behind me, causing my shadow to stretch toward it.

I took a step within the doorway, reaching for a light switch instinctively, only to find none. When I took my second step, the space lit up brilliantly.

An audience had gathered, and heads peered out on either side of me. I knew they were asking me questions, tugging on my clothing, and tapping my body, but I had no answers, and I was too captivated by what I was seeing.

"There's no one here," I said taking yet another step into the space. Any words of caution I uttered at that moment were not enough to prevent everyone else darting through the door, pushing me aside, and running through the interior in various directions, shrieking as they went. If anyone were here, I mused, *we* would be the ones caught by surprise.

"Don't touch anything!" I yelled, but by this point many of them had disappeared and I am sure that my calls would go unheeded. They'd been stuck in cars for hours and needed to get their energy out and I was too dog-tired to do anything to stop them.

"What is this place?" Joseph asked, still by my side.

"I don't know," I responded quietly. We began to walk along the corridor which followed the circle of the terrarium. I was transfixed by it. "What do you suppose is in there?" I asked him, stopping to peer into the glass. But he subtly shook his head. The mist formed drops of water on the glass, which streamed downwards. I watched them for a moment. They were hypnotic.

To our left was a door with a white hand symbol on the wall. I instinctively put my hand on the symbol, which was larger than my own, and it flashed green. The door slid open. Inside, there was a dryer and washing machine, a hamper that contained some white medical coats, and some tools. "It looks like a utility closet," Joseph said.

The corridor led into an open concept kitchen.

"Isn't this amazing?" Violet exclaimed upon seeing us. "Although, I wouldn't open the fridge if I were you," she laughed.

"I'll believe you," I said laughing as I already had caught a whiff of whatever was in there.

On the ceiling there was a large skylight, whose light cast upon the floor.

"It's not real," Joseph said staring up at it along with me.

"You're right," I said, "it's not possibly real since there is a forest directly above us and this shows a sky."

There was a dining area and a fireplace next, surrounded by a living wall, covered with various plants. We had one in the school cafeteria, but not as elaborate.

"Thyme," Joseph said smelling one of the plants.

"And mint and basil," Violet continued excitedly.

On the other side of the wall, was a living room, and as we continued around the corridor, we came to a glass elevator with a hand symbol. On the center of the door was a large rectangle and within that it had, etched in the same white as the hand, a message. Joseph read it aloud:

"CAUTION
BIOSENSITIVE AREA"

"What does that mean?" I asked.

"I don't know, but I don't think we should go in there," he responded.

I paused a moment and pressed the hand symbol anyway. It flashed red and the door didn't open. "I guess that means we aren't getting in there," Joseph said.

Behind the living room was a washroom and to our amazement showers. I suddenly felt dirty and aware of how much sweat and grime had accumulated on my body. I hadn't had a shower in weeks.

"I can't wait to get in there. I can't believe this place!" I said aloud to Joseph. "It has electricity, a kitchen, living room, showers... what is this place?"

"It's crazy," he responded.

Behind the shower, another metal door had been opened and led into a glass enclosure. Many of the kids had assembled inside. "Andrew! Look at all the fish! It's like a fish aquarium!" Luna said.

"This is the lake," I said aloud in fascination. "This is Crawford Lake. We must be under it! But how?"

Inside was a long, glass cylindrical hallway, supported by large aluminum circular beams, spaced at even intervals. The floor was made of a solid white material that had no seams and shined like glass, so much so that I could see my reflection.

The enclosure never led anywhere to the south, which I figured meant that we were at the southern-most part of the cliffs, but to the north, it continued about fifty meters to a solid metal door that was visible at the end.

"Where does that lead to?" I asked Bella who had been checking it out.

"It's locked," she responded, "there's no handle or anything."

To the west of the hallway, were three round glass rooms, each about the same size as my bedroom, although there was nothing within them and the earth, they were embedded within, was visible through the clear glass.

The sun's rays pierced through the water and lit the room an emerald tinge. Most of the kids were pressing their hands and faces against the glass and staring at the fish that swam in the clear lake. What had become of the fish in the Toronto aquarium? Dependent on humans for food and for electricity to filter the water. I shunned the thought. At least here, the fish were free. The plague did not affect them.

I had been to the lake many times, even stared into the water to watch the turtles and fish swim, and yet, never had there been any hint of what lay beneath.

This place was clearly not intended for visitors and not once had my father even mentioned it. He would disappear from home sometimes for days at a time and say that he was going to work, and then would come back for a couple of days. My mother never said anything either, but maybe she didn't know.

We left them all in the glass enclosure, and continued along the hallway, back toward the main entrance door and there were three offices to our left. The offices were made entirely of glass.

Joseph pushed the hand symbol beside one of the doors, causing it to slide open and picked up a picture off the desk, "it's you," he said, turning the picture frame toward me.

I was standing in the door frame and looked to the right of the door. It had my father's name engraved in the same semi-opaque white as the hand, 'Stuart Kirkwood'.

"Is that your dad?" he asked me. I looked at the engraving and ran my fingers along his name.

"Yeah."

"What did he do?"

I looked at him. "He was a scientist," I said stepping into the office.

"What kind of scientist was he?" Joseph asked inquisitively while looking through some papers on the desk.

"I'm not sure, he never spoke about his work."

"This isn't exactly a typical place to work."

As he reached across the desk a holographic image appeared lengthwise along its back.

"Whoa," Joseph said.

"What'd you do?"

"I just…" he said swiping his arm across the desk, which caused the image to disappear once again.

"Get it back!" I said and he swiped his arm across again causing the image to appear once more.

"It looks like a computer screen, but in the air," I said.

"Where's the mouse?" he asked, but at the same time I was poking my finger into the holographic image and as I did, an application opened on the screen.

"Cool!" Joseph exclaimed loudly. For a few minutes more, we were mesmerized, opening various applications by tapping on the holographic image. I opened one that displayed maps, charts, and various numbers.

I instinctively used my fingers to make a narrowing gesture on the map, which caused it to zoom out. "It's Canada," Joseph said as he jumped in and tried to zoom out more.

"Now, it's the World," I said laughing as it became a flat map of the entire planet. "But what are all these dots?"

At the side there was a 'house' icon, which Joseph tapped, and it zoomed the map back into a dot labeled 'Crawford Lake'. Neither of us had any answers.

We left the office and continued along the hallway. There was a small lab. I put my hand on the symbol, and it flashed red. I tried again.

"It looks like it's locked too," Joseph said.

The lab was lined with white metal benches, which were rounded at the top and bottom edges. Fluorescent lights bordered the ceiling around the top of the room. The floor was made of a white marble and was seamless.

The lab was filled with all sorts of equipment, of which the only thing I could identify were microscopes and some test tubes.

"That looks nothing like our science room," Joseph said.

"It's a pretty small lab for the size of this place," I said in response.

That night, all of us slept on the floor or on the couches, the elder of us sleeping on the latter so the younger kids could get a good night sleep. The floors were cold, and I never fell asleep until the early morning hours. I had wandered back to my father's office, sometime around two in the morning, agitated by the snores of the others and curled up under his desk. At least here it was dark and quiet, and I felt closer to him.

When I awoke, everyone was gone except for Violet, who was in the kitchen cooking lunch. I had already missed breakfast but wasn't hungry. When I didn't eat, I simply lost my appetite altogether, and I hadn't been eating well the past few days.

"Where is everyone?" I asked, but before she could answer, I heard their shrieks from the glass enclosure.

"They are all in there, looking at the fish," she replied.

"Why not go and join them?"

"Are you kidding? It's like a zoo in there," she responded.

I walked into the bathroom and removed my clothes. I had worn them for so long, they felt like they had become part of my body. I turned on the water, which heated immediately and began to shower. I must have stayed in there for at least a half-hour, sitting on the floor with my knees to my chest and letting the water pour on me like warm rain.

After showering, I realized that I hadn't brought a change of clothes into the washroom. Indeed, I had no idea whether they were brought in or whether they were still in the car. I resentfully put on my old clothes, which felt even more soiled against my clean skin.

I walked out into the enclosure, and I sat down on the concrete floor.

"We can't sleep on the floor forever," Joseph said as he sat down next to me. He was right, of course, and I imagined that he brought this up because of last night's sleeping arrangements.

"You didn't sleep either?" I asked looking at his tired face.

"Not a wink." There were a few moments awkward silence. "Where did you get to?"

"To my dad's office, under the desk. I needed quiet."

"We need beds."

"And food," I nodded adding, "there won't be enough here to last us very long."

The stark reality of the new world was becoming clear. Even if we had all stayed in one of the houses, we would still need beds, we would run out of food and need more. The question is what we would do about it.

"We need to go into the city," he said, breaking the silence.

We had just arrived and already we were speaking about going out. I found myself having the same feelings I had when pressured to go to Shelburne. I regretted that decision. This time though, we'd be splitting up. The possible outcomes were already racing through my mind causing my anxiety to flare up. I can see why my dad had us come here. It was remote, surrounded by forests and fields. It has electricity and amenities that we didn't have at home. But we'd still run out of supplies. We'd still need to leave and go to nearby towns and cities – to raid.

"I agree," I said conceding defeat. "Where will we get mattresses? How will we get them back here?" I could see my questions had him thinking, but at the same time, I realized that he was looking to me for answers.

"We can find a van, there has got to be one somewhere in the city."

"To be honest, I'm a bit scared to go back out there," I said staring at the floor.

"I am too," he said, "but you won't be alone."

It was the middle of the night when I awakened again. The darkness made it impossible to tell the time on my father's watch, which I had begun to wear on my wrist. Albeit still many sizes too large, I didn't care, and the weight reminded me of him several times each day. I didn't have anything of my mother's though, and I regretted that.

I was fine without a bed, curled up under the desk in my father's office. A floor mat I had found yesterday in the maintenance room provided sufficient cushioning and insulation from the cold floor. I drifted in and out of sleep, wakening from the same nightmares I figured everyone else had, turning from one side to the other as the one got sore.

The next time I awoke, I began to turn and realized someone was behind me, cuddling me. I could feel their breath upon my neck and heartbeat through my back. I turned my head slightly to look, but the room was too dark. I didn't need to see though; I could smell his scent on his clothing, it was distinctive, a deodorant mingled with sweat – I had noticed it before. It was Joseph.

CHAPTER

Five

Y OU WERE HAVING A nightmare", he whispered into my ear, burrowing his head in the small of my neck and nestling his body even closer to mine. I never reacted and fell quickly back asleep, not awaking again until morning.

When I awoke, he was gone. Over breakfast we decided to take Mia and drive south to Burlington. The three oldest kids leaving wasn't smart, but it was a necessity. This was something that Joseph and I couldn't do alone.

We drove south on Guelph Line, past the forests and farms, and through a small village, all of which were quiet and lifeless. The fields that once were home to cattle and sheep were now barren, and although I knew what really became of them, I chose to believe that they escaped and were free, wandering somewhere far away.

I wanted to talk to him about last night, but with Mia with us, I couldn't. He confided in Mia about what transpired when we left the city. He told a tantalizing tale so radically different from my view of events. Sure, it had all the elements, but how he regarded me was in stark contrast to how I viewed myself.

He spoke about how *I* rescued him from his condo, how *I* saved us from the three psychopaths – omitting the gory details, and how *I* safely guided us out of the city. His words not once diminishing me but overlooking his role almost entirely.

I didn't know whether to feel flattered at his kind words or disappointed at him for having such a lowly view of himself. I glanced at him through the corner of my eye as he told the story. He was laughing, albeit nervously, as he sprinkled in a bit of humor. Mia seemed completely captivated by it. I wondered if this tale would reverberate through the others when we returned home and I would then be forced to hear it repeatedly, slightly different each time. I wasn't used to hearing praise.

If it weren't for him stepping on the gas pedal, we would have probably become victims ourselves. If it weren't for him, it would have been impossible for me to navigate and even make it out of the city before nightfall. And if it weren't for him, I doubt I would have had the resolve or strength to be here at this moment. I wanted to tell him how I felt, but I would have to wait.

As we neared the edge of the Niagara Escarpment, we could see the vast expanse of Lake Ontario and the cities that surrounded it, which distracted us all from Joseph's story.

As we entered the city limits, the streets were empty and seemingly abandoned, like the old mining towns that we read about at school. It was deceivingly quiet. Inside the houses and buildings, there would be other kids, just like us. Not all of them bad, like the few we'd encountered so far. Many were probably frightened and alone. I thought of what it would have been like if I hadn't met Joseph or had my nieces and nephews, I'd be still locked inside the condo. I shuddered.

We passed several grocery stores, but we figured we would start with the mattresses.

"What about air mattresses?" Mia asked.

"They are compact," Joseph added, "easy to transport."

"We need something that will last years," I blurted out, "this isn't going to end." And at that I felt bad. They had been happy and now they seemed disheartened by my words. It was the truth though, no matter hard a pill it was to swallow. This wasn't a camping trip, the world as we knew it ended, and even I was having difficulty dealing with that. "Sorry," I muttered under my breath as I continued to drive.

We kept to the main streets. We passed convenience stores, gaming stores, toy stores, and pet shops, the latter of which I wouldn't even want to go near, for fear of what we would find inside.

"There!" Mia said pointing to a bedding store.

"We don't have a van yet," Joseph said.

"I guess we should have looked for that first," I said flatly, still disheartened by my earlier remarks. I pulled the vehicle into the parking lot and stopped in front, allowing it to idle. "I can see mattresses in there, so I guess that's a good thing," I said.

All three of us were looking around, we didn't need to state the obvious concern that we had about others possibly seeing us here. It was a persistent thought that never left my mind.

"We should pull around back," Joseph said.

"Why?" I asked.

"Just to have a look." I drove the car around the back. Besides a few garbage bins, it was vacant.

"Okay, so now what?" Mia asked.

I proceeded to drive once again to the front of the building, following the alleyway. Across the road was another strip mall. There were some cars parked in the lot, vans even, but I doubted their owners would have left their keys inside. One thing was for certain, I wasn't going to go looking for their owners.

I drove across the road to the mall and pulled around the back. "Look," Mia said pointing, but I had already seen. There was a white cargo van parked behind one of the units. I pulled up alongside and we exited the car.

There was no one around. The high brick fence that lined the back of the strip mall obscured us from view. We tried the doors of the van, and they were locked.

There was a metal door with a unit number in front of the van, however it was secured with a dead bolt, and we would not be able to open it from the outside. We would have to go into the store. "Let's go around front," I said, leading the way.

We walked around the front of the mall. I didn't like being out in the open again, unprotected. At each corner of the building, I paused a moment to survey the area.

When we reached the front, we realized that the van belonged to a pet store. My heart sank. We'd have to go into the store to find the key, and I dreaded what we might find in there.

I put my hand up to the glass and looked into the window. It was dark inside. Everything looked intact and the door was locked. Joseph walked over to a grassy area near the side of the strip mall and picked up a rock.

"Wait!" I said, standing in front of him, "it'll make noise."

"We got to get in there, there's no other way," he responded. I moved aside. "Stand back," he said as he stood in front of the door and threw the rock. The glass didn't shatter, but rather cracked.

"Great," I said throwing my arms up in the air.

He threw the same rock again and again, as I paced back and forth. A hole began to form, but it wasn't very large. The noise carried, like noise at night and there was nothing to drown it out anymore. I became worried and told him to stop.

I took off my shirt and wrapped it around my arm and hand. I reached slowly through the opening and unlocked the door. As I began to withdraw my arm, I cut it on a piece of glass.

"Ouch," I yelled, pulling it out faster.

"Are you okay?" both Mia and Joseph asked almost simultaneously.

I grabbed my arm and held it tightly as blood dripped from the cloth.

Joseph grabbed my arm, "let me look," he said as I winced. "It's not too big, but it's deep," he said pressing my shirt against the wound with both of his hands.

"Thanks," I grumbled, "at least it's open," I said nudging my body toward the door.

The three of us went inside, me last, still clutching my arm. The store was dim, lit only by the daylight coming through the front windows. I had already become re-accustomed to expecting electricity after spending only a couple of nights in the compound. No animals, I thought, looking down the aisles, breathing a sigh of relief. It was only a supply store.

"Look for the van keys," Joseph said as he went behind the front cash counter and rummaged through several of the drawers.

Mia and I walked to the back, where there was a door marked 'Employees Only'. It was unlocked, and we entered, but the interior was completely dark.

"We need a flashlight," I said to Mia and then suddenly a beam of light shone from behind us both.

"Looking for this?" Joseph asked as he handed me and Mia red flashlights with handles shaped like cats. It was then we noticed that the beam itself had a shape, like the shape of a mouse.

"Funny," Mia said sarcastically. We walked inside and all began looking for the keys. "Found them!" she declared moments later.

We walked toward the back door and opened it, stepping into the sunlight.

A German Shepherd crossed the alley about 50 yards from us, a stray, I guess. All pets that survived this nightmare, that were able to escape their homes or yards, would be strays now. I had heard from some kids at school how in Eastern Europe, pet dogs formed packs and after several generations, they were dangerous, wild-like. The dog avoided us, glancing only briefly in our direction, before disappearing behind some nearby brush. Luckily, we only had to worry about other kids for now.

Joseph started the van. It had gas, hopefully enough to get us back to the compound. I drove with Mia back to the Mattress store, with Joseph following behind us. I could see he struggled a bit maneuvering the vehicle, but he managed. I couldn't imagine. He *was* a better driver than me.

We opened the back doors of the van. Mia tried the back door of the Mattress store. "It's locked," she said annoyedly. Of course, it was locked, I thought, why wouldn't it be?

"We lucked out with the van," Joseph said as we walked around the other side of the strip mall to the Mattress store entrance.

The entrance of the door and interior was also intact.

"I guess there wasn't a rush on mattresses either," I said sarcastically.

"I'll get a rock," Joseph said.

"I've got my other arm," I said holding up my uninjured one. He grinned.

He threw the rock, but this time it smashed the glass, which fell to the ground. We all looked around nervously to see if it had drawn the attention of anyone, but there was nothing.

The entrance of the store consisted of a small showroom, with a few naked mattresses lying on bed frames. The southside wall of the store had oak shelves containing a variety of linens and pillows.

We walked to the back of the store, where rows of mattresses were lined up vertically.

"Hmm," Joseph said. It was the first noise in minutes that any of us made. There were all different sizes, from single to king, and box springs as well.

"Why don't we just take different sizes?" I said decisively. But then we continued to all stand there quiet for at least another minute.

Joseph broke the ice by reaching for the first single mattress that he could see, and I reached to help him.

"Is your arm okay?" He asked.

"Yeah, it's stopped bleeding," I said removing the cloth. "Mia, why don't you grab the linens at the front?" I asked as I tried to help Joseph slide the mattress out. The plastic cover was making it difficult to grab the mattress, but we managed.

"Which ones?" she asked.

"Let's just take all the singles," Joseph said. And that made sense to me as well, so I didn't say anything.

"Sounds good," Mia responded as she ran off to the front of the store.

We continued to drag the mattresses out of the store, loading them into the van. "Crap," I said as we tried to lift a fourth on top of the three that we already had. We had been laying them flat, and now realized that we couldn't lift them high enough to stack on top of the others.

We were both sweating, and my arm was hurting. We took a moment until Mia emerged with bags filled with linens.

"Why are you both standing there?" she asked annoyedly.

"We stacked them the wrong way," Joseph said pointing to the mattresses. He was hunched over resting his hands on his knees trying to catch his breath.

"Why don't you put them vertically," she said judging the height of the mattresses to the height of the van opening.

"We should have done," Joseph replied, and he looked at me as we began to pull them back out again. Mia had disappeared back into the store and had left several bags packed with linens and pillows alongside the van.

"Load these up boys," Mia said instructively as she emerged with even more bags. Both Joseph and I didn't argue.

"I'm starving," Joseph said.

"Me too," Mia agreed.

"We still need to get food as well," I said. We had become so focused on the mattresses that we forgot all about food.

"Maybe we can pick something up at one of the smaller stores along the way?" Mia asked.

"We will have to," Joseph said.

I thought for a minute as both Mia and Joseph looked at me in anticipation of me speaking. "We should just take the car, instead of driving around town with both vehicles," I finally said.

"That makes sense," Mia replied.

I nodded, "that's why only I will go."

Joseph looked at me, "like hell you will, I don't think you should go alone," he said. I was taken a bit aback by his response.

"It's safe here. I can stay here," Mia said.

I shook my head in protest, without saying anything and while staring at the ground thinking. "We made a lot of noise, what if someone heard?" I asked.

"She'll be okay, it's a lot riskier out there than here," Joseph said while walking to the car and planting himself in the passenger seat. It was clear, from his perspective, I wouldn't be going alone.

"Wait in the van Mia, keep low and lock the doors. If anyone comes, drive away," I said to her. She nodded and we left her there.

Joseph and I drove south along Guelph Line. I stopped at a convenience store. The windows were smashed out, and we waited a minute to listen for any noise. When we were convinced that it was safe, we went inside trying to avoid the glass at the front entrance.

The inside wasn't necessarily bare, but it wasn't well stocked either. It smelled. Flies were buzzing around the rotting sandwiches and foodstuffs in the once refrigerated displays.

We took baskets from the front entrance and began filling them with anything we could find. Produce that was still unspoiled, coconut water and sports drinks, soaps and detergents, pasta, and cans of soup, was all that we managed to scavenge. The word 'scavenge' stuck in my head. Before, we went with money to a store to buy what we needed, and now we were coming to a store and taking what was left.

The higher shelves had more food than the lower ones and often anything up there, such as crackers, we loaded up on. "I'm starting to miss vegetables," Joseph said. On any normal day, I would think he were being sarcastic, but our ability to make a healthy meal out of what we had so far in our baskets would be difficult at best.

When we reached the cashier area, most of the candy that usually lay under the counter was gone, although there were still dark chocolate bars. "I like dark chocolate," Joseph said as he stocked up on them, grabbing them by the handful. He must be the only one, I thought. Joseph then scaled the counter and grabbed some lighters, "these could come in handy," he said as he exerted himself to climb back over.

"This isn't much," I said looking down at our four baskets of food. I could see the disappointment on his face.

"We need to go to another store then," he said confidently. This food would barely last a week.

"What about Mia though?" I asked, "she would be worried about us."

He paused for a moment, and I could see him thinking. "We should go back south, pass by, and then let her know that we will be back."

"I think we should just keep going," I said, "get it over with." Driving around the strip mall might attract more attention.

"It's up to you," he said.

We put the contents of the baskets in the car, and although I was about to discard the baskets themselves, Joseph stacked them and managed to find space in the trunk of the car.

We drove further south until we came across a large grocery store. The parking lot itself was empty and I idled the car.

"Do you think it's safe?" he asked me. I rolled down the window and listened. I still couldn't get over how quiet everything had become. Except for a few birds chirping in a nearby tree, there was nothing. I felt more comfortable in the smaller store, where at least some natural light entered, and we never had to rely solely on flashlights. But this would be different, it would be like the garage in the condo.

"I think we're safe," I said in a whisper, "but we should be quick and quiet, we spent too much time in the other store." He nodded in agreement. "Where should we park?"

"I think we should park in the back," he said. I nodded and drove to the back of the store. Seeing a car in a big empty parking lot would be like putting a big red sign outside the store.

We grabbed a couple of orange stray shopping carts and went inside.

Someone had broken the glass of the automatic doors and pushed them open, leaving just enough space for us to get the carts through. As we entered, the glass under the wheels made a lot of noise and again we paused and listened. Nothing.

I began to kick the glass aside with my shoes. "No wait," Joseph said, "leave it. It will alert us to anyone else coming in." I wondered at that moment if there were people inside and they had thought the same thing. It made me apprehensive. I was glad that I never came alone.

The store itself was dark. We pulled out our flashlights and shined them around the store. There was no one, although a few birds had taken refuge in the metal rafters and flied around at the light.

The entrance led into the produce area. We grabbed anything that was packaged and produce that hadn't spoiled, mostly bags of potatoes, carrots, yams, onions, garlic, lemons, and limes.

The bakery was full of moldy breads, cakes, and muffins. Anything packaged that may have kept had already been raided. Beyond that, the smell of the meat and poultry section was overwhelming and plagued with swarms of flies and writhing maggots.

"We should stay to the interior of the store," Joseph said, "the whole outside is just freezers and fridges and it's all rotten." I didn't protest and followed his lead.

We went down the toiletries aisle and filled up a cart simply on these items alone. We found ourselves taking things we didn't even need, such as razors, but I didn't care and neither of us questioned it. I didn't want to come back here, even though I knew no matter what we took, we would run out of eventually and so would everyone else. And so, we took what was there, and even after, there was lots left.

Along the same aisle, were a lot of health foods. My mother often shopped at health food stores. She was always trying to get us to eat healthier. My dad often complained about the irony of health foods since a lot were packaged and processed and there is nothing healthy about that. Nonetheless, it seemed many shared the same opinion since the shelves were fairly-well stocked. We took cookies, oatmeal, and granola.

The next few aisles were about half depleted. We stocked up on everything we could. Cans of fish, tomatoes, vegetables, fruits, sauces, pasta, bags of rice, and after about ten minutes, we needed another cart.

Joseph went to get an empty cart, taking the one we had just filled and leaving it near the door. Him being gone, even briefly, filled me with anxiety. When he returned, we continued stuffing the cart with as much as we could find. Salt, sugar, and spices.

"What will happen when we run out of all this?" Joseph asked pausing. He stole my thoughts from just minutes before. We would run out, it was inevitable. Society had stopped. There were no operating plants, no trucks, or trains to deliver food items, so when it's gone, it won't be like we can come back and get more. And there would be nothing left by then. Others would come and plunder. Perhaps we would become like the stranger, going from house to house in the night, taking whatever was there. It was a discussion we needed to have, but not right now I thought. Not here, exposed, Mia in an alleyway, while we talk about what hasn't happened yet.

I avoided answering it by changing the subject and continuing to load the cart.

"Honey," I said, saying the first thing I saw on the shelf.

"Honey is something we could probably get wild if we needed to," Joseph said, and he was right, although I was unsure if either of us knew where to find wild honey or even how to safely collect it.

I paused and looked at him answering his question as superficially as I could, "I'm unsure, but we'll figure it out." I could tell this wasn't enough to satisfy him, but I didn't have an answer and we needed to keep moving.

When we turned down the next aisle, Joseph froze. I could tell that he had seen something, and I shone my flashlight in the direction of his eyes.

"What is it?" I asked him quietly.

"I thought I saw someone," he responded, turning his gaze at me.

I took his hand. We walked quietly around the end of the aisle and there was a boy.

"I don't want any trouble," the boy blurted out.

"We're not looking for it also," I said back. "I'm Andrew and this is Joseph."

"I'm Kevin."

"Are you alone Kevin?" Joseph responded to the boy, who was maybe eight years old. The boy shook his head. "Is there someone else here with you?" Joseph asked, as I looked around nervously. The boy shook his head again. "You seem harmless enough, do you want to come with us?" Joseph asked, "we have a safe place."

"No place is safe," the boy blurted out before running off into the direction of the store entrance.

"I think that's our cue to leave," Joseph said to me. I agreed and we both followed.

The boy had disappeared. I jogged to the back of the building and pulled the car around and we began to fill every space we could. The process of emptying the carts, became almost as time consuming as filling them. Then there was a noise in the distance.

CHAPTER

Six

Y OU WERE HAVING A nightmare", he whispered into my ear, burrowing his head in the small of my neck and nestling his body even closer to mine. I never reacted and fell quickly back asleep, not awaking again until morning.

When I awoke, he was gone. Over breakfast we decided to take Mia and drive south to Burlington. The three oldest kids leaving wasn't smart, but it was a necessity. This was something that Joseph and I couldn't do alone.

We drove south on Guelph Line, past the forests and farms, and through a small village, all of which were quiet and lifeless. The fields that once were home to cattle and sheep were now barren, and although I knew what really became of them, I chose to believe that they escaped and were free, wandering somewhere far away.

I wanted to talk to him about last night, but with Mia with us, I couldn't. He confided in Mia about what transpired when we left the city. He told a tantalizing tale so radically different from my view of events. Sure, it had all the elements, but how he regarded me was in stark contrast to how I viewed myself.

He spoke about how *I* rescued him from his condo, how *I* saved us from the three psychopaths – omitting the gory details, and how *I* safely guided us out of the city. His words not once diminishing me but overlooking his role almost entirely.

I didn't know whether to feel flattered at his kind words or disappointed at him for having such a lowly view of himself. I glanced at him through the corner of my eye as he told the story. He was laughing, albeit nervously, as he sprinkled in a bit of humor. Mia seemed completely captivated by it. I wondered if this tale would reverberate through the others when we returned home and I would then be forced to hear it repeatedly, slightly different each time. I wasn't used to hearing praise.

If it weren't for him stepping on the gas pedal, we would have probably become victims ourselves. If it weren't for him, it would have been impossible for me to navigate and even make it out of the city before nightfall. And if it weren't for him, I doubt I would have had the resolve or strength to be here at this moment. I wanted to tell him how I felt, but I would have to wait.

As we neared the edge of the Niagara Escarpment, we could see the vast expanse of Lake Ontario and the cities that surrounded it, which distracted us all from Joseph's story.

As we entered the city limits, the streets were empty and seemingly abandoned, like the old mining towns that we read about at school. It was deceivingly quiet. Inside the houses and buildings, there would be other kids, just like us. Not all of them bad, like the few we'd encountered so far. Many were probably frightened and alone. I thought of what it would have been like if I hadn't met Joseph or had my nieces and nephews, I'd be still locked inside the condo. I shuddered.

We passed several grocery stores, but we figured we would start with the mattresses.

"What about air mattresses?" Mia asked.

"They are compact," Joseph added, "easy to transport."

"We need something that will last years," I blurted out, "this isn't going to end." And at that I felt bad. They had been happy and now they seemed disheartened by my words. It was the truth though, no matter hard a pill it was to swallow. This wasn't a camping trip, the world as we knew it ended, and even I was having difficulty dealing with that. "Sorry," I muttered under my breath as I continued to drive.

We kept to the main streets. We passed convenience stores, gaming stores, toy stores, and pet shops, the latter of which I wouldn't even want to go near, for fear of what we would find inside.

"There!" Mia said pointing to a bedding store.

"We don't have a van yet," Joseph said.

"I guess we should have looked for that first," I said flatly, still disheartened by my earlier remarks. I pulled the vehicle into the parking lot and stopped in front, allowing it to idle. "I can see mattresses in there, so I guess that's a good thing," I said.

All three of us were looking around, we didn't need to state the obvious concern that we had about others possibly seeing us here. It was a persistent thought that never left my mind.

"We should pull around back," Joseph said.

"Why?" I asked.

"Just to have a look." I drove the car around the back. Besides a few garbage bins, it was vacant.

"Okay, so now what?" Mia asked.

I proceeded to drive once again to the front of the building, following the alleyway. Across the road was another strip mall. There were some cars parked in the lot, vans even, but I doubted their owners would have left their keys inside. One thing was for certain, I wasn't going to go looking for their owners.

I drove across the road to the mall and pulled around the back. "Look," Mia said pointing, but I had already seen. There was a white cargo van parked behind one of the units. I pulled up alongside and we exited the car.

There was no one around. The high brick fence that lined the back of the strip mall obscured us from view. We tried the doors of the van, and they were locked.

There was a metal door with a unit number in front of the van, however it was secured with a dead bolt, and we would not be able to open it from the outside. We would have to go into the store. "Let's go around front," I said, leading the way.

We walked around the front of the mall. I didn't like being out in the open again, unprotected. At each corner of the building, I paused a moment to survey the area.

When we reached the front, we realized that the van belonged to a pet store. My heart sank. We'd have to go into the store to find the key, and I dreaded what we might find in there.

I put my hand up to the glass and looked into the window. It was dark inside. Everything looked intact and the door was locked. Joseph walked over to a grassy area near the side of the strip mall and picked up a rock.

"Wait!" I said, standing in front of him, "it'll make noise."

"We got to get in there, there's no other way," he responded. I moved aside. "Stand back," he said as he stood in front of the door and threw the rock. The glass didn't shatter, but rather cracked.

"Great," I said throwing my arms up in the air.

He threw the same rock again and again, as I paced back and forth. A hole began to form, but it wasn't very large. The noise carried, like noise at night and there was nothing to drown it out anymore. I became worried and told him to stop.

I took off my shirt and wrapped it around my arm and hand. I reached slowly through the opening and unlocked the door. As I began to withdraw my arm, I cut it on a piece of glass.

"Ouch," I yelled, pulling it out faster.

"Are you okay?" both Mia and Joseph asked almost simultaneously.

I grabbed my arm and held it tightly as blood dripped from the cloth.

Joseph grabbed my arm, "let me look," he said as I winced. "It's not too big, but it's deep," he said pressing my shirt against the wound with both of his hands.

"Thanks," I grumbled, "at least it's open," I said nudging my body toward the door.

The three of us went inside, me last, still clutching my arm. The store was dim, lit only by the daylight coming through the front windows. I had already become re-accustomed to expecting electricity after spending only a couple of nights in the compound. No animals, I thought, looking down the aisles, breathing a sigh of relief. It was only a supply store.

"Look for the van keys," Joseph said as he went behind the front cash counter and rummaged through several of the drawers.

Mia and I walked to the back, where there was a door marked 'Employees Only'. It was unlocked, and we entered, but the interior was completely dark.

"We need a flashlight," I said to Mia and then suddenly a beam of light shone from behind us both.

"Looking for this?" Joseph asked as he handed me and Mia red flashlights with handles shaped like cats. It was then we noticed that the beam itself had a shape, like the shape of a mouse.

"Funny," Mia said sarcastically. We walked inside and all began looking for the keys. "Found them!" she declared moments later.

We walked toward the back door and opened it, stepping into the sunlight.

A German Shepherd crossed the alley about 50 yards from us, a stray, I guess. All pets that survived this nightmare, that were able to escape their homes or yards, would be strays now. I had heard from some kids at school how in Eastern Europe, pet dogs formed packs and after several generations, they were dangerous, wild-like. The dog avoided us, glancing only briefly in our direction, before disappearing behind some nearby brush. Luckily, we only had to worry about other kids for now.

Joseph started the van. It had gas, hopefully enough to get us back to the compound. I drove with Mia back to the Mattress store, with Joseph following behind us. I could see he struggled a bit maneuvering the vehicle, but he managed. I couldn't imagine. He *was* a better driver than me.

We opened the back doors of the van. Mia tried the back door of the Mattress store. "It's locked," she said annoyedly. Of course, it was locked, I thought, why wouldn't it be?

"We lucked out with the van," Joseph said as we walked around the other side of the strip mall to the Mattress store entrance.

The entrance of the door and interior was also intact.

"I guess there wasn't a rush on mattresses either," I said sarcastically.

"I'll get a rock," Joseph said.

"I've got my other arm," I said holding up my uninjured one. He grinned.

He threw the rock, but this time it smashed the glass, which fell to the ground. We all looked around nervously to see if it had drawn the attention of anyone, but there was nothing.

The entrance of the store consisted of a small showroom, with a few naked mattresses lying on bed frames. The southside wall of the store had oak shelves containing a variety of linens and pillows.

We walked to the back of the store, where rows of mattresses were lined up vertically.

"Hmm," Joseph said. It was the first noise in minutes that any of us made. There were all different sizes, from single to king, and box springs as well.

"Why don't we just take different sizes?" I said decisively. But then we continued to all stand there quiet for at least another minute.

Joseph broke the ice by reaching for the first single mattress that he could see, and I reached to help him.

"Is your arm okay?" He asked.

"Yeah, it's stopped bleeding," I said removing the cloth. "Mia, why don't you grab the linens at the front?" I asked as I tried to help Joseph slide the mattress out. The plastic cover was making it difficult to grab the mattress, but we managed.

"Which ones?" she asked.

"Let's just take all the singles," Joseph said. And that made sense to me as well, so I didn't say anything.

"Sounds good," Mia responded as she ran off to the front of the store.

We continued to drag the mattresses out of the store, loading them into the van. "Crap," I said as we tried to lift a fourth on top of the three that we already had. We had been laying them flat, and now realized that we couldn't lift them high enough to stack on top of the others.

We were both sweating, and my arm was hurting. We took a moment until Mia emerged with bags filled with linens.

"Why are you both standing there?" she asked annoyedly.

"We stacked them the wrong way," Joseph said pointing to the mattresses. He was hunched over resting his hands on his knees trying to catch his breath.

"Why don't you put them vertically," she said judging the height of the mattresses to the height of the van opening.

"We should have done," Joseph replied, and he looked at me as we began to pull them back out again. Mia had disappeared back into the store and had left several bags packed with linens and pillows alongside the van.

"Load these up boys," Mia said instructively as she emerged with even more bags. Both Joseph and I didn't argue.

"I'm starving," Joseph said.

"Me too," Mia agreed.

"We still need to get food as well," I said. We had become so focused on the mattresses that we forgot all about food.

"Maybe we can pick something up at one of the smaller stores along the way?" Mia asked.

"We will have to," Joseph said.

I thought for a minute as both Mia and Joseph looked at me in anticipation of me speaking. "We should just take the car, instead of driving around town with both vehicles," I finally said.

"That makes sense," Mia replied.

I nodded, "that's why only I will go."

Joseph looked at me, "like hell you will, I don't think you should go alone," he said. I was taken a bit aback by his response.

"It's safe here. I can stay here," Mia said.

I shook my head in protest, without saying anything and while staring at the ground thinking. "We made a lot of noise, what if someone heard?" I asked.

"She'll be okay, it's a lot riskier out there than here," Joseph said while walking to the car and planting himself in the passenger seat. It was clear, from his perspective, I wouldn't be going alone.

"Wait in the van Mia, keep low and lock the doors. If anyone comes, drive away," I said to her. She nodded and we left her there.

Joseph and I drove south along Guelph Line. I stopped at a convenience store. The windows were smashed out, and we waited a minute to listen for any noise. When we were convinced that it was safe, we went inside trying to avoid the glass at the front entrance.

The inside wasn't necessarily bare, but it wasn't well stocked either. It smelled. Flies were buzzing around the rotting sandwiches and foodstuffs in the once refrigerated displays.

We took baskets from the front entrance and began filling them with anything we could find. Produce that was still unspoiled, coconut water and sports drinks, soaps and detergents, pasta, and cans of soup, was all that we managed to scavenge. The word 'scavenge' stuck in my head. Before, we went with money to a store to buy what we needed, and now we were coming to a store and taking what was left.

The higher shelves had more food than the lower ones and often anything up there, such as crackers, we loaded up on. "I'm starting to miss vegetables," Joseph said. On any normal day, I would think he were being sarcastic, but our ability to make a healthy meal out of what we had so far in our baskets would be difficult at best.

When we reached the cashier area, most of the candy that usually lay under the counter was gone, although there were still dark chocolate bars. "I like dark chocolate," Joseph said as he stocked up on them, grabbing them by the handful. He must be the only one, I thought. Joseph then scaled the counter and grabbed some lighters, "these could come in handy," he said as he exerted himself to climb back over.

"This isn't much," I said looking down at our four baskets of food. I could see the disappointment on his face.

"We need to go to another store then," he said confidently. This food would barely last a week.

"What about Mia though?" I asked, "she would be worried about us."

He paused for a moment, and I could see him thinking. "We should go back south, pass by, and then let her know that we will be back."

"I think we should just keep going," I said, "get it over with." Driving around the strip mall might attract more attention.

"It's up to you," he said.

We put the contents of the baskets in the car, and although I was about to discard the baskets themselves, Joseph stacked them and managed to find space in the trunk of the car.

We drove further south until we came across a large grocery store. The parking lot itself was empty and I idled the car.

"Do you think it's safe?" he asked me. I rolled down the window and listened. I still couldn't get over how quiet everything had become. Except for a few birds chirping in a nearby tree, there was nothing. I felt more comfortable in the smaller store, where at least some natural light entered, and we never had to rely solely on flashlights. But this would be different, it would be like the garage in the condo.

"I think we're safe," I said in a whisper, "but we should be quick and quiet, we spent too much time in the other store." He nodded in agreement. "Where should we park?"

"I think we should park in the back," he said. I nodded and drove to the back of the store. Seeing a car in a big empty parking lot would be like putting a big red sign outside the store.

We grabbed a couple of orange stray shopping carts and went inside.

Someone had broken the glass of the automatic doors and pushed them open, leaving just enough space for us to get the carts through. As we entered, the glass under the wheels made a lot of noise and again we paused and listened. Nothing.

I began to kick the glass aside with my shoes. "No wait," Joseph said, "leave it. It will alert us to anyone else coming in." I wondered at that moment if there were people inside and they had thought the same thing. It made me apprehensive. I was glad that I never came alone.

The store itself was dark. We pulled out our flashlights and shined them around the store. There was no one, although a few birds had taken refuge in the metal rafters and flied around at the light.

The entrance led into the produce area. We grabbed anything that was packaged and produce that hadn't spoiled, mostly bags of potatoes, carrots, yams, onions, garlic, lemons, and limes.

The bakery was full of moldy breads, cakes, and muffins. Anything packaged that may have kept had already been raided. Beyond that, the smell of the meat and poultry section was overwhelming and plagued with swarms of flies and writhing maggots.

"We should stay to the interior of the store," Joseph said, "the whole outside is just freezers and fridges and it's all rotten." I didn't protest and followed his lead.

We went down the toiletries aisle and filled up a cart simply on these items alone. We found ourselves taking things we didn't even need, such as razors, but I didn't care and neither of us questioned it. I didn't want to come back here, even though I knew no matter what we took, we would run out of eventually and so would everyone else. And so, we took what was there, and even after, there was lots left.

Along the same aisle, were a lot of health foods. My mother often shopped at health food stores. She was always trying to get us to eat healthier. My dad often complained about the irony of health foods since a lot were packaged and processed and there is nothing healthy about that. Nonetheless, it seemed many shared the same opinion since the shelves were fairly-well stocked. We took cookies, oatmeal, and granola.

The next few aisles were about half depleted. We stocked up on everything we could. Cans of fish, tomatoes, vegetables, fruits, sauces, pasta, bags of rice, and after about ten minutes, we needed another cart.

Joseph went to get an empty cart, taking the one we had just filled and leaving it near the door. Him being gone, even briefly, filled me with anxiety. When he returned, we continued stuffing the cart with as much as we could find. Salt, sugar, and spices.

"What will happen when we run out of all this?" Joseph asked pausing. He stole my thoughts from just minutes before. We would run out, it was inevitable. Society had stopped. There were no operating plants, no trucks, or trains to deliver food items, so when it's gone, it won't be like we can come back and get more. And there would be nothing left by then. Others would come and plunder. Perhaps we would become like the stranger, going from house to house in the night, taking whatever was there. It was a discussion we needed to have, but not right now I thought. Not here, exposed, Mia in an alleyway, while we talk about what hasn't happened yet.

I avoided answering it by changing the subject and continuing to load the cart.

"Honey," I said, saying the first thing I saw on the shelf.

"Honey is something we could probably get wild if we needed to," Joseph said, and he was right, although I was unsure if either of us knew where to find wild honey or even how to safely collect it.

I paused and looked at him answering his question as superficially as I could, "I'm unsure, but we'll figure it out." I could tell this wasn't enough to satisfy him, but I didn't have an answer and we needed to keep moving.

When we turned down the next aisle, Joseph froze. I could tell that he had seen something, and I shone my flashlight in the direction of his eyes.

"What is it?" I asked him quietly.

"I thought I saw someone," he responded, turning his gaze at me.

I took his hand. We walked quietly around the end of the aisle and there was a boy.

"I don't want any trouble," the boy blurted out.

"We're not looking for it also," I said back. "I'm Andrew and this is Joseph."

"I'm Kevin."

"Are you alone Kevin?" Joseph responded to the boy, who was maybe eight years old. The boy shook his head. "Is there someone else here with you?" Joseph asked, as I looked around nervously. The boy shook his head again. "You seem harmless enough, do you want to come with us?" Joseph asked, "we have a safe place."

"No place is safe," the boy blurted out before running off into the direction of the store entrance.

"I think that's our cue to leave," Joseph said to me. I agreed and we both followed.

The boy had disappeared. I jogged to the back of the building and pulled the car around and we began to fill every space we could. The process of emptying the carts, became almost as time consuming as filling them. Then there was a noise in the distance.

CHAPTER

Seven

THE EMERALD-GREEN LAKE WAS clear and glasslike, occasionally shimmering in the sunlight whenever there was a breeze. I looked down from the cliff on which I stood. Limestone rocks jutted out from the cliffs and quickly gave way to the unseen depths below. The rocks were covered in plants and algae, which when mixed with the color of the limestone and water, gave them a yellow appearance. Small fish stayed in the relative safety of the shallows, darting inward when larger fish would emerge from the depths.

I sat on the rocks above the compound, although one wouldn't know it even existed from the surface. I thought of all the times my family visited here and not once did my father mention it, all the while knowing what lie beneath the lake. Behind me there was a boardwalk, which surrounded the lake, although we didn't use it. Instead, we hopped over the fence and walked through the forest to get to and from the compound entrance.

The kids played nearby. Mia and Bella had decided to take a walk around the boardwalk. I had let them. Mia needed a break from watching the little monsters anyways and I figured it was safe.

The boardwalk was designed to keep visitors out of the surrounding forest, to preserve the nature. Near the mouth of the lake, the walkway ceded at a small beach, although swimming wasn't allowed – I'm unsure why, perhaps for the same reason.

It had five square observation decks spaced throughout. My favorite was on the other side of the lake, near the beach. I used to climb the railing and sit on the cliff, like how I was now, but the view was much better, especially at sunset.

Madison came and sat beside me. She was seven. She had blue eyes and straight, long, blonde hair, although her teeth were rotting from years of neglected dental hygiene, which I am sure many of us were guilty of at this point.

"What have you got there?" I asked her curiously.

"I'm making a fishing rod," she said in her tom-boyish voice.

"What?" I asked in astonishment, reaching for the stick, and holding it in the palms of my hands. I eyed the stick end. "Where did you find this hook and line?" I asked gently handling it.

"I found it down there", she said pointing toward the observation deck nearest us. There was a certain irony in that fishing wasn't allowed within the lake either.

"This is a great idea," I said, smiling as I handed her back the stick. "All you need now is some bait," I laughed.

"I have that too," she said reaching into her white dress pocket and pulling out a couple of earth worms. I laughed.

I helped her secure a worm on the hook, although I was probably more squeamish than she. Madison dropped her line into the water, and we peered over the edge.

"You need a longer stick," I said, "the smaller fish are just nibbling at your bait." I climbed over the boardwalk fence and into the nearby forest and selected a longer branch. I broke off the twigs as I brought it back and helped her re-fasten the line.

Minutes after putting it back into the water, she had caught her first fish. "Hang on tight," I said as I helped her hold onto it. Still not very big, and I hadn't a clue what type of fish it was, it was something, and a brief sense of normalcy fell over me. I had never been fishing before, and I doubt Madison had either.

Our cheers attracted the attention of some of the other children, seeing that we were relatively quiet until then. The fish floundered on the rock beside us, until it seemingly gave up. It wasn't long before we had caught a second and third fish.

"There you are," Joseph announced, coming up behind us and putting his arm around my shoulder.

"We're catching fish," Madison said gleefully to him while she kicked her legs back and forth over the edge of the cliff.

"You are?" he asked in a playful voice.

"We caught three," she said. I put my hand on her back, somewhat anxious that she was so close to the edge. I had no idea if she could swim. I couldn't.

"I have something to show you," Joseph said.

"Let's get these fish back inside then," I said to Madison, helping her up after getting up myself. We looked down at the fish and realized we had nothing to carry them back with.

"Okay then!" I proclaimed, "this fish is for you," I said picking up a fish and handing it Madison, and "this fish is for you," I said handing another to Joseph, and "this fish is for me," I said picking up the last fish. I hollered to the other kids, and it wasn't hard getting them to come back inside since they were all interested in the fish we were holding.

Back inside, we put our catch into the kitchen sink. Violet was unimpressed by this since she had never had to clean a fish before. I felt bad but we all left her to it.

Joseph led me to the terrarium. When no one was looking, he pressed his hand against the symbol next to the door and it slid open.

CHAPTER

Eight

H OW DID YOU DO that?" I asked in astonishment, "it was locked before."

"You know the computer in your dad's office?"

"Yeah."

"It had an app for that," he said, and we both laughed.

When we entered, the door closed behind us, and we found ourselves in an elevator. It was completely glass, although the surrounding air was so full of mist that it was impossible to see anything. As it began to descend, the mist lessened and more of the terrarium was revealed. I was glued to the glass, captivated already by the little that I could see.

The elevator doors opened, and we found ourselves in a room. Within the room was another door with a sign in the same white as everything else. It read:

CAUTION

BIOSENSITIVE AREA

REMOVE ALL CLOTHING

AND SHOWER BEFORE ENTERING

Joseph began removing his clothing.

"Can't we just go in?" I asked, reaching for the hand symbol next to the door. But when I pressed it, it flashed red before turning white again.

"You don't have permission yet," Joseph said smiling still removing his clothes.

"Have you already been in there?" I asked him, suspecting that he had from the grin on his face.

"Yup," he said smiling.

It concerned me that if something had happened to him, no one would have known. But I couldn't think with him removing his clothes in front of me and he was naked before I had even begun.

"Well?" he asked looking at me. I felt rather uncomfortable removing my clothes.

"Oh, alright!" I said reluctantly and in a minute I too was naked.

He placed our clothes on a glass shelf and pressed a white shower head symbol on the wall.

A fierce wind blew within the chamber, from a vent in the ceiling, and was sucked into the metal grated floor.

"What kind of shower is this?" I yelled, struggling to keep my balance. Then water sprinkled from the ceiling. "Ah!" I screamed, "it's cold! How do you turn it off?" I yelled looking around the walls.

"It will go off itself," Joseph yelled back chuckling.

When the water subsided, the door in front of us opened and it let out a welcome burst of warm, humid air. Joseph led the way, "come on," he said beckoning me. As I entered, I was awestruck by the enormity of it all. What was immediately evident was that the size of the enclosure above us paled by what lay beneath.

Behind us, the elevator door closed and was seemingly invisible from the outside, resembling the surrounding vegetation.

In front of us was a white glass pathway, that went from the elevator door and followed the circle of the terrarium as far as I could see.

We walked along the pathway, which oddly wasn't slippery, even with all the condensation that formed droplets everywhere, including on my skin, which refused to dry.

The path was surrounded by flora that blocked the view of the glass walls, which I assumed were there, perhaps hidden by the same technology as the elevator door.

Some of the plants I recognized, bromeliads and orchids. A coconut that had fallen near the path edge, led my eyes upward to the tree it fell from, whose top vanished within the fog.

Birds sat singing in the trees, while others darted through the foliage from limb to limb, occasionally flying in front of us. Others hopped along the ground, digging their beaks within the soil searching for what I could only imagine were insects or seeds. Vibrant colored butterflies softly glided from flower to flower sucking their fragrant nectar.

An azure-colored frog with a light body and dark legs clung to the underside of a large leaf, its shadow giving away its presence.

"Isn't that poisonous?" Joseph asked.

"I dunno, but let's not touch it," I responded cautiously.

We continued along the path as it spiraled around in a clockwise direction.

We stopped at a spring from which crystal-clear water gushed from the ground and sat on the large rocks that lined the edges. Younger trees covered with lichen and moss as well as shrubs, surrounded the edges, allowing a certain amount of light to penetrate through the canopy.

Small bubbles emerged from the sandy substrate of the turquoise water. The water formed small waterfalls that flowed over large rocks and filled other pools before disappearing in the understory.

I cupped my hand and drew some water.

"No, no, no!" he yelled in concern as I drank from my hand.

"It's okay, it's right from the ground."

"How does it taste?"

"Like water," I responded and then he took some as well.

I poured some on my face and body, wiping away what had changed from condensation to sweat.

A green iguana was resting against a small tree and, save for its eyes, it didn't move, and we didn't bother it.

I touched the rock upon which I sat with my fingers.

"It's real," I said in disbelief.

"Yeah," Joseph responded.

"I mean, it's actually real."

"It's not like the exhibits at the zoo," Joseph responded solemnly. No those were completely fake I thought, but this was real.

Even fallen trees lay along the edge of the stream. Leaves and bark covered the rocks. Even the roots of trees were intertwined within the rocks. "They built all of this. I mean we are underground," I said still astonished by it all. "There's more," Joseph said standing up, "come on."

The path slowly descended further, and I realized that we were on an embankment, eventually giving way to a large body of water. A waterfall fell from a rock face covered with vegetation. The water was clear and deep with a white sandy bottom, visible in the shallow areas.

Giant lily pads with high edges floated on the surface. Fish swam beneath the path and emerged on the other side; it was as though we were floating.

The path led to a round platform in the middle of the water. From which extended a metal spiral staircase with white glass steps reaching upward.

"If it weren't for the path, we could be anywhere," I said to Joseph.

Then thunder, and it began to rain from a sky that did not exist, from which there were no clouds. It spit at first and then began a downpour, such as that I could not see even an arms-length from my face. "How?" I yelled. "Hurry," Joseph yelled, grabbing my hand as we climbed the stairs upward.

After a long climb, they led to a closed metal door which, when Joseph opened, revealed a small, all-glass, dome. We scrambled inside, where it was dry.

Around the edges was floor seating and both of us sat down, shivering. Joseph put his arms around me. "To keep warm", he said, sensing my hesitation in letting him.

"It's the forest," Joseph said, his teeth chattering as he turned to look outside the dome. I was inattentive to our surroundings, unfocused on anything other than getting warm. We were above ground, within the forest that surrounded the lake. I wondered if anyone who passed by would have seen the dome. Certainly, employees of the conservation lands would have come across it. Why everything else being so well hidden, was this so obvious?

He turned from the window to face me. I looked at him, at his face and eyes. He smiled and intentionally blinked both his eyes at me. I felt exposed, once again aware of my nakedness. It made me uneasy, and I wanted to cover myself, but there was nothing to do so with. I just sat there silently, trying to avoid looking at him and to not look as awkward as I felt.

I am sure that if I weren't shivering, I would have turned several shades of red. There was nothing in the room to distract us, nothing to use as a topic for conversation and my mind was so occupied that I couldn't think of anything else.

The sound of the rain subsided and for me it was a relief. I stood, and him with me. We climbed back down the stairs into the humid air. I once again felt cloaked in a blanket of warmth. We walked back along the path to the elevator, never speaking. I tried to look at the surroundings, seemingly occupied, but my mind was unable to stop thinking about him.

I picked up the fallen coconut. I shook it and the water inside swished around. I glanced at him, and he was smiling at me. We got dressed and returned up the elevator to the compound.

"Where were you guys?" Mia asked when we walked into the kitchen. Luckily no one had seen us enter or leave and I didn't want to tell anyone where we had been.

"The fish smells great," I said avoiding her question. I put the coconut on the counter and lied that I had found it in one of the offices. Violet was frying the fish. "It doesn't look like much," I said. They had shrunk as they cooked. Her eyes opened wide as she glared at me. I felt as though her head could have come off her shoulders and rotated mid-air at my remarks. I immediately felt bad and left the kitchen.

We all congregated in the living area and ate. Once I finished, I went to stay by myself in my father's office and sat in his chair. I didn't know what any of it meant. The compound, the terrarium, my feelings for Joseph. It had been wearing on me. I curled up under his desk and cried myself to sleep.

That night, Joseph never came. I had begun my previous regiment of tossing and turning from one side to the next, hoping that the next time I turned, he would be there. I even thought at one point of faking some groaning sounds to see if he would re-appear. But he did not. The next day, his behavior did not change, he would come sit near me at meals, he would smile, but both of us would largely remain quiet, keeping our conversations short and focused on daily problems.

I would find myself looking at him and when he would catch me, he would smile, and I would look away. The nights passed and he did not come back, and I felt at a loss. One day, I was walking along the boardwalk, and he came running behind me, placing his hands on my shoulders, and trying to get me to give him a piggyback. Of course, I couldn't, at least not very long. He was laughing and bantering about.

Then he looked into my eyes and leaned into kiss me quickly near my mouth. I didn't move. His laughter abated and he leaned in again a second time, but this time kissed me briefly on my mouth. He didn't close his eyes and neither did I. Indeed, I couldn't take my eyes off him.

He then wrapped his arms around me and held me. I reached up and did the same. His heart was beating fast, and so was mine. He then moved his arm around my shoulder and motioned me to walk with him around the boardwalk. He didn't say anything about what just occurred and neither did I. We spoke about all the goings on, the others, all as though nothing had happened.

That night, I couldn't see him when I retired. I wondered if he were outside or had found a place to sleep somewhere else. I said my good nights to the few who were awake and retired to the office. When I reached the desk and knelt, he was there, lying on his back staring up at me in the subtle light.

He smiled. His hands were resting on his chest and his knees were up off the floor, the area was much too small to lie flat and as I crouched down beside him, he turned me to face the opening of the desk and nestled his body once again into mine, grasping me tightly with his arms, holding my hands with his own.

He kissed the back of my neck, and it sent a tingling sensation all over my skin. I didn't know how to feel, only that how I did feel, felt right, and that I didn't want to lose it.

CHAPTER

Nine

I WAS AWAKENED BY a commotion. Not the typical hyperactivity or hostility between kids fighting over the last remaining candy, but the alarming sound of distress. I heard my name repeatedly and I quickly sat up, hitting my head on the bottom of the desk.

"Ouch," I yelled, which roused Joseph who was still sleeping beside me.

"You okay?"

"Yeah, I'm alright," I bemoaned, holding my fingers against the back of my head, and checking for blood.

"Let me see," he said, trying to look as we both sat in the confined small dark space under the desk. I didn't complain but the angle I was sitting at was hardly comfortable or conducive to the task.

Moments later, Mia hurried in, "Andrew, you need to come quickly," she said as I looked up at her and scowled, massaging the top of my head which was already starting to form a painful bump.

"You okay?" she asked.

"I will be if everyone stops asking me that," I mumbled as I crawled out from under the desk with Joseph behind me. "What's happening?"

"The front door was open, and Chloe was gone," she said.

We ran to the front door, which was slid open, and looked out in the parking lot. It was empty, except for our cars.

"Mia, Daniel, Joseph, come with me, the rest of you stay here, no one leaves, I'm sure she can't be far," I said as we ran outside. "Mia and Daniel, you look near the lake, Joseph and I will follow the road."

We left in pairs and as we got some distance, I could hear Mia and Daniel begin to call out Chloe's name. Not wanting to attract attention from passersby, neither Joseph nor I did the same. I wish I had told them to look quietly, but now I could only hope for the best that they wouldn't be heard.

We both looked at the ground for footprints, and the tree line for any signs of disturbance as we walked down the road toward Guelph Line. There was no one around and nothing seemed out of place.

I tried to stay calm as we walked briskly, my eyes frantically checking everywhere for any clues of her whereabouts. I felt a wall of anxiety. I couldn't lose Chloe or anyone else for that matter.

Joseph then stopped for a moment and placed his arm against my stomach motioning me to do the same. There she was, just north of us toward the swamp, with her back facing us, almost obscured by some branches that lay near the road. We ran up behind her calling her name, "Chloe, Chloe." Joseph ran in front of her and after giving a quick look over, held her in his arms.

When I saw her face, she was largely despondent. Even the embrace of Joseph did little to alter her stare. I traced her eyes and, in the brush, not more than twenty meters away, was a car.

"Joseph, look." He turned to look in the direction I was pointing. "Stay here," I said as I began to walk toward the car, but he picked up Chloe and carried her, following slightly behind.

The engine of the car was still warm, and it had been covered with brush. I tried the door, but it was locked. I looked at Joseph, "someone was here recently," I said. "Chloe, did you see anyone?" I asked her, but she turned her head into Joseph's neck and put her arms around him. "We need to get back immediately," I said. And both of us walked as quickly as possible back to the compound.

"Mia, Daniel," I whispered under my breath. I felt panicked, I couldn't leave Joseph behind as he carried Chloe, but in the distance their hollers could still be heard and if we could, so could whoever had been driving the vehicle.

"They are giving away our position," Joseph said. "Go find them and we will head straight to the compound."

"I don't like leaving you both alone."

"We'll be okay," Joseph said reassuringly.

"Argh," I moaned feeling conflicted, glancing at him before running in the direction of their shouts.

Joseph knew I was a fast runner. The entire school did. I had won first place several years in a row, except this year, when I had tripped seconds after the race started and tied for third. I wasn't good at long distances, but my strong legs and light body, allowed me to excel with short bursts of power. It was about the only athletic thing I was good at, and it probably had more to do with genetics than any sort of conditioning.

I felt free when running. I felt like all my problems left me, and the rush of wind against my body gave way to a feeling that I was the wind itself. The rest of the world disappeared, while I focused on what was in front of me. In this case though, I was focused on reaching Mia and Daniel.

I ran into the forest, avoiding the parking lot. The rocky ground slowed me down and the slippery moss made it hazardous, but within minutes, I could see Mia and Daniel in the distance.

I began to wave my arms in the air, without speaking, hoping they would notice, but it was the sound of breaking twigs under my feet that drew their attention.

"Be quiet," I whispered as I reached them. I looked around, tuning out their questions. "Quiet," I said again.

"What's wrong?" Mia asked also in a whisper.

"We found Chloe, but there is someone else here," I said in a low voice. "We need to be quiet and get back to the compound immediately."

We walked quickly and in a couple of minutes, we had reached the door. "Is he here?" I blurted out distressed as we entered. Upon seeing Joseph, I was relieved. He was sitting beside Chloe who was lying down on the living room couch. "I'm so glad you're safe," I said. I hated leaving him alone on the road and I wanted to embrace him, but that would have to wait.

"Did you see anything?" He asked.

"Nothing."

"Neither did I."

I took a moment and paced a bit, much to the concern of my onlookers who remained silent. I put my hand to my forehead, I was getting a headache. I hadn't even eaten yet, and I was unsure if any of us had.

"Can someone cook something already?" I asked frustratingly. Violet left the room and started rummaging through the kitchen. I could tell she was upset, and this only frustrated me further. I paused and looked at everyone. "No one leaves anymore, you all need to stay inside. I'm serious!" I shouted.

I went to the office and sat under the desk. I felt bad for yelling and even worse knowing how Violet would take my comment. As if she should be solely responsible for feeding the lot of us! A few minutes later Joseph brought me some food and sat down in front of me. "I just needed some space," I said. "I didn't mean to yell."

He put his hand on my shoulder and then put some food up to my mouth. I took a bite. This was the first time anyone had ever put food in my mouth, except maybe my parents. I chewed. It was good. I had no idea what it was, but it was good.

"Violet made it yesterday," he said. I slumped my head down in my arms feeling ashamed of myself.

"It's okay. They understand," he said. "We all understand. We're all safe inside."

I nodded while I gathered my thoughts. "It's not that. Whoever was in that car, probably already knows we are here. They would have heard Mia and Daniel yelling and they probably have seen our cars and the door of the compound," I said emotionally. "I mean, I don't know if we are safe. It's just a door." I paused and calmed down a bit. "We need to find whoever is out there, and when we do, deal with them."

"Deal with them?" Joseph asked inquisitively. I think he was surprised by my words.

"We need to figure out their intentions," I said choosing my words more carefully. He nodded. "Then we need to do a better job of hiding our presence," I continued, "the cars, the door, the parking lot."

"How do we hide a parking lot?" he asked. He was right, I had no idea.

He put more food in my mouth. The effects started to make me feel better. Not great, but better. Whatever bread like substance he was feeding me was going straight to my head. Not only the food, but I was glad *he* was here. When we finished, he stood up and reached for my hand to help me up. "Well then, let's go find these strangers," he said.

The compound had no windows. No real ones anyway. Everything, even the skylight in the kitchen, was superficial. I still hadn't figured out why this was. We had no way to see outside, no way to determine who was on the other side of the door. For all the technology in this place, it seemed like a massive blunder.

I took some paper from the office desk and a pen and wrote on the paper: '1. Need to see outside.' I folded the paper and put it with the pen in my pocket.

"Stay inside," I said to everyone, as Joseph and I went to the door. I took the paper out of my pocket apologizing as I wrote a second item on my list: '2. Need a second exit.' We needed other ways of getting in and out of the compound, otherwise, it could become a prison. Even rabbits had more than one hole to their burrow.

Joseph could see what I was doing. "I like it," he said with a smile that I modestly returned.

We could have used a second exit right about now. We were about to exit the compound through a door, that was visible from a wide-open space –

the parking lot. This gave our adversaries an advantage. They could watch us from the tree line, and we wouldn't even know they were there. They may have been even watching us this morning.

I opened the door and stayed within the darkness of the cave. I scanned the tree line with my eyes. The wind made it difficult. Every bush that moved, every tree that swayed, I had to keep refocusing.

"We don't even have a weapon," I whispered to Joseph who stood behind me. That should be item three on my list, I thought, but I made a mental note and left the paper and pen within my pocket.

I took Joseph by the hand and made a bee line toward the forest where I could better assess the surroundings. "Perhaps we should wait here," Joseph said. I looked at him, and he could tell the puzzled look on my face needed him to explain further. "Well, whomever is out there, should have heard Mia and Daniel, and they would have followed their voice, perhaps even seen you running back or me returning with Chloe. They are probably watching the compound, perhaps even where we are right now."

As he spoke, I began to move both of us backward further into the tree line. He was right, he didn't even have to finish. I pointed toward the other side of the parking lot, to the edge of the forest, near the road, a shadow amongst the bushes. I gently moved his head in the direction of my finger. "There," I said.

CHAPTER

Ten

I T WAS HARD TO make the boy out. He was around our age, of medium build, but it was impossible to tell anything else at this point, such as the color of his hair or eyes.

"We need to move to a different position," Joseph said. And he was right. The stranger noticed us leave, knew where we were at, but didn't know we were aware of him.

We moved up the ridge above the compound, careful to not make any noise. Joseph picked up some evergreen branches and handed me some. "Hold these in front of you," he whispered.

We looked back in the direction of the stranger.

"He didn't see us move," I said, as he was still in position, looking back toward where we entered the forest.

"What do we do now?" Joseph asked me.

"I was going to ask you the same thing," I smirked quietly.

It was almost noon, none of us were moving, and the only thing that was, were our stomachs.

"What if there's more than one?" Joseph whispered. It was possible I thought.

"Let's hope not," I whispered back.

"We need to do something though, we should split up," he said and before I could interject, he continued, sensing I would refuse any such idea. "One of us could distract him, while the other closes in on him."

My eyes looked downward from his face as I thought. At least it was a plan, what other option did we have?

I looked back into his eyes, "the way we snuck out of the compound, he must either believe that we know someone is out here, or he is waiting to see if more people come out and how many there are of us."

"He is trying to figure out what he's up against. Or maybe he wants to know if we're a threat to him?"

"That's possible too."

"It would be great to have the power to read minds," Joseph said with a mild chuckle. I agreed with him there, I would love to know what he was thinking about me.

Everyone was always treating me like the leader, always asking me what we should do, and I didn't want to be the only decision maker. Joseph was smart and I trusted him.

"Would it be wrong for me to say, I think you should lead on this one?"

"Sure," he said smiling, "anything for you." He pointed, "so you're fast. You should go around to get closer to him – not too close." I could sense his concern. "But close enough that if he runs or engages, that you could catch up to us quickly. Meanwhile, I'll exit the forest where we came in, and I'll announce that I know where he is."

I nodded and pointed to a couple of bushes within sight, "I will wait there, watch for me."

I walked deeper into the forest, to ensure that the stranger could not see any movement. I picked up a heavy stick on the ground and walked across the top of the compound, mindful that there may be others.

The stranger was no longer in sight, and neither was Joseph. But I continued with the plan. It was difficult to know which bushes I had been pointing to, once I was in the thick of the forest, but I stopped when I was about half-way the length of the parking lot.

Moments later, Joseph walked out of the forest. At first, he didn't let on anything and began walking toward one of the cars, but then he looked over at me and then to the end of the parking lot in the direction of the stranger.

"I see you there," he hollered. "I'm unarmed, and you have nothing to fear from me."

"Where's the other?" a deep voice asked back.

"He is in the forest, gathering berries," Joseph yelled back convincingly.

I could hear the snapping of branches from where the stranger sat, and moments later, he emerged into view, walking toward Joseph. He had dark hair and although his eyes were not visible, they too were dark, possibly brown. He was taller than Joseph as well and, in his hand, he carried a metal bar.

"I'm unarmed," Joseph said again, putting the palms of his hands out in a non-aggressive stance. "What's your name?"

"Brad," the boy said. "How many of you are there?" He asked. His voice gave away a slight aggression, but perhaps it was fear.

"Would you tell me if you were in my shoes?" Joseph asked.

"No," Brad replied with a bit of a chuckle.

"How did you find us?" Joseph asked. I wondered why he didn't ask Brad to drop the metal bar and it was making me nervous. I could feel the edge of my toes ready themselves to run to his aid and at this distance it would take me about three seconds to get there. Would that be enough time? I wanted to get closer, but I couldn't take my eyes off them, besides, this is where I agreed to stay.

"My car ran out of gas," Brad replied. I couldn't tell if he was lying. But what were the odds?

"Why stay in the area though? There's nothing here."

"Obviously," Brad replied, raising the bar to point toward the compound. The soil loosened under my feet at the movement of the bar and had me ready to lunge.

"We don't want any trouble, we're peaceful," Joseph said.

"How can I trust you?"

"I'm unarmed, and you're still holding that metal bar."

"I've only seen five of you, and you look the oldest," Brad said, still somewhat aggressively. "I could take all of you."

I didn't like his response, but his tone had a slight restraint. "I know you don't want to do that," Joseph replied.

"Have you been to the city?"

"We have."

"Then you know what things are like there, it's everyone for themselves."

His face had become flush, he was growing angrier, and Joseph had stepped back slightly. It was his hand though that made me react. I could see it tighten on the end of the bar. I didn't waste any time, I lunged forward from the brush, sprinting straight toward Brad.

CHAPTER
Eleven

O NE, I COUNTED IN my head, Joseph stepped backwards a few steps. Two, Brad looked in my direction toward the sound of my feet rapidly approaching him. The energy had welled up and I am certain my face had turned purple from the surge of blood as I propelled forward. Three, he didn't even have time to raise his bar, as I lunged through the air and knocked him off his feet.

The metal bar fell from his hand, and Joseph came to pull me off him, realizing that the boy had been knocked out cold as he fell to the ground.

"He's passed out," Joseph said, helping me off the ground, "are you alright?" The adrenaline rushed within my body, and it took me about a minute of pacing to calm down. I was shaking. I nodded, as I tried to catch my breath.

I picked up the metal bar and held it, but no sooner had I done that, Joseph took it gently from my hand and threw it toward the forest.

"We are peaceful," he said to me.

I nodded at Brad's body. "He's not though," I said angrily. "He could have hurt you with that bar."

"But he didn't, I had you to save me," he said calmly with a smile.

I stopped pacing. "What do we do with him before he wakes up?"

"I never thought that far ahead in the plan."

"Can we pick him up?" I asked, trying to lift his legs.

"We wouldn't want to take him into the compound, would we?"

"I don't think it's a good idea."

"At this point, he doesn't know what's in there, how many there are of us, he knows very little, it's best we keep it that way."

"I wonder if we can tie him up."

"Let's say we do that, we tie him up, what do we do with him then? At some point, he is going to need to be untied."

"Maybe it will give us time. We can check his car and see if he was telling the truth about the gas and send him on his way," I said.

Joseph jogged back to the compound and came back with some packing tape a minute later. "This is the best we have," he said handing it to me.

I began to tie his hands first. I put his wrists together and wrapped the tape around them and then in between them. I then tied his feet and knees in the same manner. Joseph just watched.

About fifteen minutes later, Brad began to wake up. At first, he was startled, and tried to unfree his hands by biting the tape, "Don't do that," I said sternly, and he stopped.

"We are peaceful," Joseph once again repeated.

"I wasn't going to do anything," Brad said.

"I don't believe you," I interjected angrily. Joseph looked at me, and I could sense his displeasure, so I walked a few feet away and sat down sulkily on the ground with my arms across my knees. His expression changed slightly; he was pleased with my decision to let him handle this. We were developing an understanding for one another.

"Brad, we need to know what to do with you," Joseph continued. "We can give you some gas, you could get in your car, and drive somewhere else, but my," and Joseph paused, "partner here is worried you will just come back with others." I thought of his choice of word. He didn't say friend, he said partner.

"But I am an understandable guy, you could stay here, with us, join us." At this I perked up, but I trusted Joseph and didn't interrupt. Joseph looked at me to see my reaction. "Do you have any skills?" Joseph asked him.

"I can hunt," Brad said.

"You couldn't even see us, and you were unaware of me, and you say you can hunt?" I protested. I could tell once again from Joseph's face that he was displeased, however, he agreed in principle with my question and continued.

"My partner has a point," Joseph said. There was that word again, 'partner'.

"You're right, I couldn't see you," Brad said defeatedly, "but I can set snares and catch rabbits. It's how I've been surviving."

"Go on," Joseph said giving him an upward nod.

"I left the city a couple of weeks ago. The gangs there got so bad. I took a car and have been driving north along with the exodus."

"The exodus?" Joseph asked as we both leaned forward curiously.

"Yes, kids are leaving the cities, the dead, the flies, the gangs, and moving into the woods. You don't know?"

"I mean, no," Joseph responded.

"How did you find us though?" I asked. We both looked at Brad, who had managed to sit up, even though he was bound.

"It was by chance."

"By chance?" I asked in disbelief, standing up from my seated position.

"Every night, I just pull my car off the road, down a driveway or into a field, cover it up, and I stay for a few days until I see others and then I leave."

"But you didn't leave when you saw us," I asked.

"My car ran out of gas," Brad said again.

Joseph stood. Brad looked scared at this point as both of us stood above him. All the anger and aggression had gone and even his size didn't intimidate me anymore. Joseph looked at me, and without any words, I nodded back at him.

"You will come and live with us," Joseph said. "Do you want that?" It didn't take any time before Brad nodded.

I knelt and began removing the tape, first from his feet, then knees and then from his wrists. Joseph reached down and held out his hand to Brad, who took it and stood up.

"Sorry about the tape," I said.

"I would have done the same thing," Brad replied.

"We will come with you to your car," Joseph said.

I was starving and my energy was low. Whenever I am hungry, I get grumpy. When I'm hungry and tired, I get even grumpier. I took some gas from the trunk of our car, and we walked back to Brad's car. He had an older car, a beaten-up silver Ford Escort. He pulled the branches off the car.

"Do you mind if...?" I asked, as I put my hands out for him to throw his keys.

"Sure," he said throwing me the keys, which I caught. I opened the driver side door and put the key in the ignition, watching him around Joseph out of the corner of my eye. Trust had to be earned. He was right, it was out of gas. I popped the fuel door and Joseph poured some of the gas into the car. I turned the engine and it started. Joseph got in the back, and Brad got into the passenger side, and we drove back to the compound.

When we reached the parking lot, I popped the trunk as Joseph and Brad got out. In the back there were three snares, just like Brad had said. I put the gas can in the back, took the snares, and went inside with Brad and Joseph.

When we entered the compound, everyone inside looked as shocked as Brad.

"You have power?" Brad asked.

"We have everything," Joseph said. "I will show you around and introduce you."

I went into the office and left the three snares on, what had now become, my desk. I reached into my pocket, unfolded the paper, and wrote '3. Weapons'. We may be a peaceful people, but if it is true what Brad said, if there was an exodus coming, we would need to defend ourselves, and not just against one person, but entire gangs.

That night, we found Brad a place to sleep in one of the other offices. And Chloe of all the kids had oddly taken a liking to him. She stayed near him, and he to her.

"She reminds me of my little sister," Brad said.

I could sense sadness in his voice. "Where is she?" I asked him.

"If you don't mind us asking," Joseph interrupted.

"It was the virus."

"But she was younger?" I asked.

"Some kids die too. There are bodies of children all over the city."

"So, this is what happened to Ava and Hannah," I said looking at Joseph.

"Who are they?" he asked.

"Don't worry, get some sleep," I said, and we left him be.

He earned some trust today, I thought, and Chloe fell asleep beside him as she clutched her doll. I nodded and both Joseph and I went to the office. I could see Brad watch us and I wondered what he thought when both of us disappeared under the desk. I didn't care though.

"We did well today," Joseph said as he positioned himself in front of me with his back toward my chest. He took my arms and wrapped them around him, and I held him tight as we both fell asleep.

The next morning, I realized something was missing from my desk – the snares. And when I looked around, I realized, Brad was gone. For the next thirty minutes, we ruminated over where he might be. His car was still in the lot. I wondered if it had been a good idea to allow him to join our group in the first place. We searched the compound thoroughly and there was no sign of him. No sooner had I sat down on the living room sofa, we heard a knock at the door.

"It's me," Brad said in a muffled voice from behind the metal. Joseph opened the door. "I was setting snares," he said, removing his shoes. He seemed completely oblivious to the worry that he caused. He went to lie down near the couch in the living room without even batting an eye. "There will be rabbit tonight," he muttered, before falling back asleep in a near instant.

I rolled my eyes and left the living room in frustration. I stood in the glass enclosure and stared at the fish in the lake. Joseph came up behind me and put a piece of food in my mouth, which I gratefully ate. It was becoming somewhat of a routine. Me forgoing eating, until he would feed me.

"What are we starting at, aşkım."

"Aşkım?" I repeated.

"It's Turkish."

"Well, I don't speak Turkish," I responded blatantly.

"It's rather difficult to learn," he said.

"I'm sorry," I said turning to him. I felt bad the way that I spoke to him just now and I felt worse that I kept apologizing for everything. "I'm just frustrated that Brad had disappeared this morning, and he's..." I tried to think of the word as I trailed off.

"Clueless?" Joseph said, nodding his head with a wide grin, on the brink of laughter.

"Yeah, that." I said grinning, looking around to see if we had been in the earshot of anyone.

"I was thinking of addressing number two on the list today," I said trying to change the subject.

"And what was number two again?" he asked resting his head on my shoulder, still with his arm around me.

"We need a second exit."

He removed his arm and began rubbing his chin with his hand. He was thinking and staring up the ceiling.

"We should go outside and look, try to find the place where it makes sense for an exit to be," he said after a few moments.

"Yeah, and how easy it would be to break through as well."

We walked to the front of the compound and carefully opened the front door. I had begun watching the tree lines, always wondering if anyone else might be watching. Brad came up behind us, "it's safe out, I was just out checking the snares," he said startling us.

As we walked out the door, he asked us, "is there something I can do?"

"Four," I replied.

"Four?" He asked inquisitively.

"Yes," I said pulling the folded paper from my pocket, "you said there is an exodus. We need to find a way to hide the front of the compound, the cars, even the parking lot."

"We need to become invisible," he said finishing my sentence.

"Yeah, pretty much," I laughed.

Joseph and I walked along the side of the compound and entered the forest. "We're going to have to do something about taking the same path. We're eventually going to form trails and these trails will make it evident that there are people," I said. Joseph just nodded. We continued walking the same path anyway, up to the boardwalk, above the compound and the glass enclosure. Another item for the list I thought.

"I wonder how they did that?" I asked Joseph.

"Did what?" he asked as he chucked a stone into the lake.

"The glass enclosure, it is completely invisible beneath us."

"There's only one way to find out," he said removing his clothing. He was stark naked before I realized what he was doing. He climbed over the boardwalk railing and jumped into the lake. He disappeared beneath the surface and came up, smiling.

"Come in," he said with a wide grin on his face.

"I can't swim," I said.

"What? You're eleven!"

"Just never got around to learning," I replied. I felt bad in a way, because I wanted nothing more than to be in that lake with him, besides, the water looked good. "Is it warm?" I asked trying to change the subject.

"I will teach you," he said, unwaveringly. "Oh, and yeah, it's damn well freezing," he said with another laugh.

"I'm definitely not getting in there then," I chuckled back.

"You're right about the path," he said while treading water. "It's just that's the easiest way for us to get to here." I looked across the lake as the winds gentle breeze caused the surface to be rougher than usual. "Maybe we can cover it regularly with twigs and leaves or drag some branches across the entrance," he said still treading. I nodded and grinned at him. The latter made a lot of sense.

He then dove back under the water, and I could see his body rather clearly. He looked like he was resting on a ledge beneath the surface and moments later he came up again. He wiped the water from his eyes and pushed back his hair.

"It's coated with something," he said, "that's why we can't see it. Not unless you're close."

"Like in the terrarium?"

"Yeah," he nodded. "The kids were all waving to me from the enclosure," he said laughing before diving back down again. Moments later he came back up. "You should be in here with me," he said when he emerged.

"You do realize you're naked, right?" I asked him. He looked confused at first, and then realized that everyone in the enclosure could see him.

"I didn't even think of that," he replied nervously.

"It's a good thing that we are not in there together," I said.

"We'd put on a real show," he replied laughing. I blushed.

He swam over to where the observation deck was, and I helped him out of the water. He began shivering, and I first used the palms of my hands to begin wiping the beads of water from his arms and chest and then removed my shirt so he could dry off. He got dressed and we were once again standing on the boardwalk, his arm around me. It was then that we saw it.

CHAPTER

Twelve

THERE WAS AN AREA where the limestone gave way to form an indent in the ground. It was just off the boardwalk, only a few meters from where we were standing. I climbed under the railing as Joseph watched. And I used my hands to remove the twigs, leaves, and dirt from the hole. The hole was about half a meter in width and would be enough for most of us to fit through. I continued to dig with my hands until the dirt got too thick.

Joseph had since come beside me. He handed me a stick as I continued to dig. He was sitting on his feet with his knees up to his chin, and the edge of his shirt collar in his mouth, intently watching me. Eventually, I hit rock again, or so it seemed.

"This isn't rock," I said, as I pulled out a few silvery pieces. "It's concrete."

"The top of the compound?" Joseph asked.

"It must be."

"We need tools, we will have to go into the city again," he continued.

"But the exodus," I said.

"We haven't seen it Andrew, and we need to understand what we're up against." It made sense. I nodded.

We decided to take Brad. He was resistant at first, saying that he was worried about going back to the city, but Joseph stoked his ego by telling him that his knowledge was important, and he agreed.

He said that it would best to leave at night, when most kids would be sleeping, and we would have the advantage of darkness as cover. Both Joseph and I agreed, and after telling the others, we laid down for a nap.

"By the way, I'm okay with the two of you," Brad said to me as I lay beside Joseph. I had no idea what he was talking about. "My cousin's gay, and love is love," he said, before turning over and facing the wall.

Gay. I hated that Brad dumped that on me. That was the word that would keep me awake for the next few hours while both Joseph and Brad slept soundly. My mind was racing. Was I gay? I thought to myself, was Joseph?

I never put a name to my feelings for Joseph. What I did know is that I never felt such a tremendous care for anyone before. For the first time, I watched him sleep. He snored lightly, not like the annoying bear-like sounds that were emanating from Brad, but calming, peaceful. I held him tighter, and the snoring stopped briefly as he talked to himself for a moment. His words were indiscernible. Whatever it was I felt for him, it felt right.

The moment in the parking lot, when Brad was seemingly ready to attack him, solidified how I felt. Before that, the kisses, the hugs, the soft whispers, they were nice, they made me feel good, but never were my feelings so clear than at that moment. He had gone from being someone who I never spoke to at school or in the elevator, to someone I couldn't see myself without.

A few hours passed and I sat up and at that Joseph began to awaken. I was always nervous when I slept during the day, and now I was nervous that I had not slept.

He wiped the sleep from his eyes. "Did you sleep?" he asked.

I just shook my head. "Sleeping, eating, who needs those?" I said with sarcasm.

I put my hand on his head and pushed back his hair, which had stuck up a little at the back. He smiled and kissed my arm briefly.

"You guys should get a room already," Brad said annoyedly. Both Joseph and I laughed, having been unaware that he too had awoken. The three of us stood up and started our drive to the city.

Burlington was about forty minutes south of Crawford Lake, maybe shorter if we drove faster, but it was dark outside and the lights on the car were off.

For the first little while, we never saw anyone. Then in the fields, in the distance, we could see fires burning and shadows moving around them. The exodus was real.

As we drove closer to the city, the number of fires and people visible in the fields grew and as we hit the city limits, we could see a roadblock in the distance.

The width of Guelph Line had been obstructed by wooden logs and a couple of burn barrels were aglow, their flames reaching up into the night sky. The smell of burning timber permeated the air. At least four kids were visible and were carrying weapons of various forms, at least one, a shotgun. We were probably a few kilometers away when I stopped the car.

"What is this?" I asked.

"It's a roadblock," Brad said.

"I can see that," I replied, "but two weeks ago, this wasn't here."

"It's the gangs. The older kids recruit the younger kids. The city is becoming full of them, which is one of the reasons I left."

"So, what are we going to do?" Joseph asked.

It became apparent at that moment that, while we had remained rather invisible up to this point, one of the kids in the roadblock had made us out. We were too far for them to reach us, even with a gun, but they began to yell for others.

I turned the car around, which wasn't as simple as in the parking lot. Although there were several lanes, I was apprehensive about ending up in one of the steep ditches. I drove for a way, parked, and then turned on the interior light. I took the map from the glove compartment and began looking for our position.

"The roadblock is…" I mumbled, allowing myself to trail off.

"Just north of Dundas," Brad said completing my sentence. He had his arms rested across the back of both of our seats as he leaned forward. His head rested on his hands, where his fingers were intertwined. "We are here," he said pointing on the map. I handed it to him. "I don't need this," he said, "I used to live just that way," nudging his head. "We can go back to the First Side Road, which is North of here." I turned off the car light and began driving again.

"Where would we find a hardware store?" I asked him.

"No," he said, "the big stores are looted. We need to think of other places where no one would go."

"Such as?" Joseph asked. I had stopped the car once again and we turned our heads to look at him.

He thought a moment. "A garden store," he replied.

I tensed my lips and gave a nod of approval to both him and Joseph. We drove westward along First Side Road. The road winded and curved at places through fields but there were no roadblocks and after a few minutes on the left-hand side, we came across a nursery.

The place was largely intact, I guess the end of the world didn't exactly beckon people to garden stores. Except for some cacti, any flowers and plants inside had long wilted, and the smell of the plants, along with the flies they attracted, was pungent enough to weaken our stomachs.

"Let's just get the tools," Brad said.

But Joseph stopped him. "Yes, I mean, but there are seeds here."

"And?" Brad asked.

"We could use the seeds to grow vegetables," I said, clueing Brad into Joseph's idea.

We grabbed several shovels, but then also loaded up the car with rakes, plastic planter boxes, every package of every seed we could find, and some bags of soil, even though we figured that would be the last thing we needed.

In the end, the trunk was full, and Brad had little space to fit in the backseat. "This is the last time I travel to a garden center with you two," he quipped and the three of us laughed. We drove back along First Side Road and northward back to the compound, leaving the exodus behind us.

When we reached the compound, I slowed. While the exodus may have been still to the south, Brad had reached us, and I was worried there may be others. We parked the car and unloaded it into the compound trying not to awaken anyone. We then ate rabbit and went to sleep ourselves.

The next day, I was eager to use the tools to try to dig through the top of the compound. We told everyone to stay out of the glass enclosure and both Joseph and I went to the boardwalk, to the hole, and began shoveling and hammering through the concrete. It was tough going.

"I think we underestimated the tools we needed to do this," I said to Joseph dismayed.

I took turns with the shovels and hammers. The hammers helped to break apart the concrete and the shovels helped to remove the fragments.

"How thick do you think it is?" Joseph asked. But I didn't have an answer. And then we hit the rebar.

"There's metal!"

"I've seen that before," Joseph said, "in the city, when they build buildings." I then realized that I too had seen it before.

We managed to continue to chip through until we saw the first light of the compound below. We could hear the concrete falling on the floor beneath us and some of the kid's voices.

"Guys, I told you to stay out of the glass enclosure," I hollered below, and they all ran away screaming.

"I wonder if they even realize it was you," Joseph said. I rolled my eyes.

We continued through the day to widen the hole until all that was left was the rebar. "Any one of us could fit through if it weren't for the bars," I said frustratedly. In a sense, if it weren't for the bars, I would feel uneasy even sitting on top of the compound now, seeing the hole and the height of the drop to the floor below.

"How are we going to get rid of these bars?"

"You need a torch or a saw," Brad said. He scared both Joseph and I again, angering Joseph slightly, which was a rarity.

"Don't keep sneaking up like that!" I yelled.

"Sorry," Brad said kneeling beside us.

"I heard your voice earlier and I decided I would come up and check it out. The kids were all screaming and thinking that a monster had been speaking with them, it was too much." I don't know why, but I felt bemused and laughed nervously.

"Where would we get a torch or a saw?" I asked. Brad looked deep in thought.

"We'd have to go out again," Joseph said.

"If we knew about this problem last night..." Brad started.

"But we didn't. Did we?" I interrupted, getting mildly upset.

"It's okay," Joseph said trying to calm me down.

"It's just that we will always run into this problem. The world has changed. We will always need something, and we can't keep going into the city with the way things are."

I stood up and walked away toward the nearest observation deck. I sat on it with my arms resting on the middle beam of the rail and legs dangling over the edge above the water. I wiped away some tears, unable to cry because of anger.

A few moments later, Joseph came. He sat beside me in the same way but rested his head on his arms and looked at me. I wiped away some more tears, while looking at him quickly.

He looked concerned. And then I felt his hand on my back, gently rubbing it and he moved closer to me. He put his other hand on my chin and gently turned my head. "No," I said starting to cry. But he was persistent, "it's okay," he said. He took the lower part of his thumb and wiped away the tears from both my cheeks and I stopped crying and looked into his eyes. "I hate seeing you sad, we're going to get through this."

"How can you be so sure?" I asked.

"Because I have you, and you have me aşkım," he said, and he pulled my body closer to him and held my head on his chest.

"What does aşkım mean?" I asked, my voice slightly muffled, still with my head on his chest.

He paused a moment, long enough that I thought he wouldn't answer. "My love," he said. I looked at him and for the first time I saw him blush. He looked sad even. As though saying what he felt made him more vulnerable than all the actions he showed until today. I smiled slightly at him, and he grinned back.

I then looked back toward the mouth of the lake. A white stork was perched in the shallows, and then it took flight, flying upward. I stood up quickly, so quickly, that I must have scared the crap out of Joseph. My mouth couldn't even form words.

"What is it?" Joseph asked as he stood up.

"The visitor, the visitor center," I said excitedly pointing toward the mouth of the lake.

"What visitor center?" he asked.

"There is a visitor center at the mouth of the lake, up a short trail. I can't believe how stupid I've been," I exclaimed. Joseph looked confused. "In all the time we've been here, we have never gone past the boardwalk around the lake, we never went to the visitor center!" I took Joseph by each of his upper arms. "There are tools," I said calmly and focused. "I mean there have to be!" I said grabbing one of his hands and running with him in tow. Joseph was not as fast a runner as I, so we did more of a jog than a run.

When we reached the mouth of the lake, we climbed the steep and winding incline up toward the visitor center.

"Wait," he said, stopping us as it came into view. "What if there are people there?" I must admit I was almost a little irate at him since I was in my moment of elation, but he was right.

"You're right, we can go slow, we will watch for a bit," I said. He nodded.

We kept to the tree line and watched the windows and doors. The building was made of a light-colored brick with a light brown roof and green trim around the eavestroughs. Above the door was a sign that read, 'Visitors Center.' The building had two levels, the lower of which we were looking at.

After we were sure that there was no movement, we tried the lower set of doors, but they were locked. We peered inside, and there was no one visible. "Stand aside," I said to Joseph as I took a rock from the side of the building and threw it through the window. The glass shattered and we once again listened for sounds. There was nothing.

We walked inside, this time, not avoiding the glass in the doorway. We looked around the lower level, which had a museum and washrooms, and found a utility closet that contained tools, a torch, a hacksaw, a ladder, but also some things that we already had, a hammer, shovel, and wheelbarrow.

I led Joseph up the stairs, where there was a gift shop. This too, I had forgotten about. Inside, were drinks, candy, clothing, jams, and other items. I grabbed some bags from behind the counter and began filling them.

"We can get this stuff later," Joseph said.

"I don't want to risk it, with the exodus. I don't want to ever leave again without taking advantage of what we have been given," and at that, he agreed and began filling bags as well.

We packed up everything we thought might be important, leaving behind useless touristy items, such as snow globes and fridge magnets.

We walked down the stairs, pulled out the wheelbarrow and filled it with the items and tools. We had too many bags to make a single trip, so we took as much as we could.

Joseph helped me get the wheelbarrow down the steps, and I pushed it down the hill while he carried some bags.

We walked along the boardwalk to the hole.

"Hey," I yelled down the hole, at which point some of the younger kids left the glass enclosure screaming once again.

A moment later, I heard Mia near the hole, "you're scaring the kids, you know that, right?"

"I have something that will change that," I said, "here catch!" and I dropped a maple leaf sucker down the hole.

"Where did you get this?" Mia gasped.

"I have a lot more, but I need you and Violet to come and get these bags and take them into the compound. Then I need you to go to the visitors center and get the other bags we left there."

"What visitor center?" Mia asked.

"It's a long story, but it's there, along the boardwalk and up the trail. Go now and watch out for strangers." Mia left the view of the hole, as I hollered after her, "and tell the kids to stay out of the glass enclosure!"

I looked at Joseph who was already lighting the torch. He passed it to me. I guess he was as eager to get this done as I was. I began putting the heat on the first of the two metal bars. As close as I could to the concrete. We looked away from the light, peering only briefly at times to see how things were progressing. After a minute the metal became a reddish glow and then lighter and then Joseph hit it with a hammer, and it snapped.

We then did the same to the others, until all the bars had been cut.

"We did it!" Joseph exclaimed.

"We just need something to cover the hole now," I said.

"We can do that tomorrow," he replied as he grabbed some evergreen branches and put them over the hole. "This will disguise it for the time being." I nodded and we began putting the tools into the wheelbarrow.

It was rough going getting the wheelbarrow over the rocks to the entrance of the compound and most of the way we carried it, me at the handle end, and Joseph at the front.

When we reached the compound door, the kids were largely silent, for once I thought, eating the candy that we had found at the visitor's center.

"Take it easy on the candy guys," Joseph said.

"None of them will sleep tonight," I joked, realizing that the joke would be on us since we wouldn't get any either.

Even Brad and the older kids were eating candy bars and drinking pop.

"Save some of that for us too," Joseph said, sitting down on the sofa and patting a place beside him for me to sit. I just watched for a moment and let out a deep breath. A feeling that we were going to be alright settled over me.

The next day, Joseph and I spent working on the second exit. We smoothed the edges of the concrete hole as best we could. We picked up the old ladder from the visitor's center so we could use it to climb in and out. It was a bit shaky, but it was the best we had.

When it began to rain later that day, we realized that we would need something snug to fit into the hole to stop rain, snow, and even insects and other critters from getting into the compound.

Joseph had the idea of using a piece of wood from the visitor's center and cutting it into a circle slightly larger than the hole. We cut the edge of a spare tire and fastened the rubber to the wood with nails. Since it stood out like a sore thumb, we disguised it by nailing evergreen branches to its surface and smearing the wood with the black mud that lined the shores of the lake.

I sat in the glass enclosure and watched as the rain drops hit the surface of the lake. I had never seen such a thing from below. I used to sit on the balcony and watch the lightening over the city. Perhaps that is what I would be doing now, if it weren't for all of this. My mom and I would be sitting on the balcony eating salad and watching the rain.

CHAPTER

Thirteen

Brad had caught a live rabbit and it was all the rage. He had fashioned a trap out of some chicken fence wire he found in the forest, or at least so he was telling me, and he wanted to keep it to breed.

"What are we going to do with it?" I asked almost defeatedly, stroking my forehead while staring at the cage feeling that this would become my undoing. Several questions raced through my mind. What would it eat? Who would clean it? Everyone had gathered around and was looking at it with awe.

"Does it bite?" Luna asked inquisitively.

"It's not a pet guys! It's wild and probably has fleas," I said annoyedly trying to subdue the cauldron of emotions I was feeling.

"It doesn't bite," Brad said answering Luna ignoring me entirely.

"Can we, can we just go..." my voice trailed off.

Joseph had been behind me, and I was so caught up in everything that he continued my sentence. "Let's go into the office Brad and talk, you can bring the rabbit."

"Awe, can't you leave it here for us?" Madison whined.

"Nope, the rabbit comes with us," I said firmly.

When we were in the office, we closed the door, but the kids were pressing their faces against it, and whatever patience I had left vaporized like the fog of their breath on the glass.

"Okay," I said taking a deep breath trying to collect my thoughts, "you want to breed them and keep them."

Brad seemingly impervious to my temperament, interrupted. "Especially with the exodus, it makes catching rabbits difficult."

I took another breath, "okay, the part I don't understand though, is where are we going to keep the rabbits, because they can't stay in the compound." Brad understood and his mouth opened as though he were going to say something, but then he quickly closed it.

"This is how the outbreak started in the first place," Joseph continued.

"Well, not with Rabbits," Brad interjected, and I put my hand against my face, which caused him to stop talking once again.

"We understand that Brad, but we can't have animals, their waste..." Joseph started, "the smell" I chimed in, "living in the same quarters as the rest of us. It's dangerous."

"We're not saying you can't keep it, and well, breed it, it's even kind of cute, it's that we need a place to keep them outside of the compound," I said.

I could see that Brad was dismayed, but I didn't care. It was a matter of health.

I believed that was the end of it, the rabbit was out of the compound for the time being. But within a day, another rabbit appeared, and then another. And then a chicken, and then I thought I was going to completely lose it.

That night, when I went to sleep, even Joseph was getting frustrated, "one thing is for certain, Brad is really good at catching rabbits," he said.

I nodded my head and replied sarcastically, "yeah, and now chickens."

"It's a great idea, but he is spending more time catching rabbits than building a place to keep them," Joseph continued.

It was this night that I had a dream, I say dream, however, I never slept the whole night because my mind was racing about everything. When Joseph began to rise, I turned to him and faced him. He was surprised since he was always the first one up.

"Did you sleep?" he asked me.

"Of course not," I sighed. "Last night was all rabbits, chickens, Brad disappearing, Brad coming back," I paused hoping he'd get my joke, but he didn't laugh. "You said last night that Brad is really good at catching rabbits, but not at building a place to put them."

"Something like that, yeah," Joseph responded.

"We are all really good at something. Brad is good at catching Rabbits, Mia at taking care of the kids, Violet at cooking, you at leading..."

"Me at leading?" Joseph interrupted and I could sense he was pleased with the recognition.

"Yes, you are a very good leader and I respect your decisions," I said.

At this he put his head on my chest, "awe shucks," he said in a bashful voice. I never told him this before and it meant something to him.

"I am apparently not good at telling people what they do well," I laughed.

He let out a chuckle. "You are good at being focused on what needs to be done," he said, "you don't have time to give praise," he continued, "you are busy just trying to keep us all alive and safe. It's all you think about."

It's not all I think about, I thought. I kissed him on the head. He raised his hand and parted the hair from my forehead. I could see the love in his eyes as he looked at me.

"The thing is, not everyone has a job and none of the kids are learning, we don't have school, for instance," I continued.

"I think we just haven't had the opportunity to think ahead," Joseph replied.

"Hmm," I moaned in agreement.

"So, you're right Andrew. We need to give people jobs," Joseph said.

One of the offices had become our hoarding stash. Much of what we didn't have immediate need for, we had stored in that room. I emerged from the office and strode into the living room with my hands full of seed packets, which I put down on the coffee table.

"Everyone, gather around," I hollered, and after a few minutes when everyone was present, I continued. "Do you know what these are?" I asked openly.

"Seeds," Bella declared.

"Yes. But does anyone know what these seeds grow into?" Daniel sat closer to the coffee table and rhymed off some of the packets, "tomatoes, strawberries, carrots." He would have continued if I didn't stop him.

"Yes, but what is the problem here?" I asked. The room was silent and after about a minute, I rephrased the question. "Where are the seeds?"

"They are on the table," Daniel responded.

"Yes, they are still in packets, on the table. We haven't planted them."

Joseph, realizing where I was going with this, glanced at me, and chimed in, "the reason that they are still in packets is because no one has taken on the responsibility of planting them. Brad, what would you say that you are good at?"

And he responded just as Joseph had wanted, "catching rabbits, I guess."

"Yes," Joseph exclaimed, "I don't know where you learned it from, but you are amazing at catching rabbits!"

"Madison is great at catching fish," I said.

"Violet is great at cooking," Joseph said.

"Well," Violet began to say modestly.

"But you are," Joseph said, "and we are all grateful for it."

"Essentially, every one of you have found a way to support us," I said. I realized that some of the kids were looking sad that they were not recognized, and Joseph had sensed this. This was definitely a strength of his.

Joseph left the room, and in a minute, he came back with some paper and pens. He began to fold and tear each piece of paper into six pieces. Some of the other kids began to help.

On each piece, he began to write a job.

"Animal Husbandry" he said as he wrote.

"How did you think up that word?" Mia asked with a laugh.

"One of my cousins is a farmer," Joseph said with a grin. "Gardening," he wrote on another, "Cooking," he wrote on a third.

"Construction," I said as he reached the fourth piece.

"Construction," he said, sounding it out as he wrote it.

"Teaching," Mia said.

"Yes!" Joseph exclaimed and she smiled, since his excitement gave her some sense of recognition. And after about five minutes, he had a stack of jobs for lack of a better word.

"Now the hard part," he said. "We need to put names on each of these pieces of paper."

"Can only one name go one a piece of paper?" Bella asked.

"No, several of you can write your name on one piece of paper, and you can also write your name on more than one, but try to limit it to one, something you feel you are, or would be really good at," he said.

"What if we change our mind?" Daniel asked.

"You can change at any time, but I want you to really think what it is you want to do," Joseph responded.

I realized at this point it would be impractical for the younger children to participate, but I felt that it would do no harm if they did, and in-fact might encourage them.

He laid out the pieces of paper on the coffee table.

"What if there is something that is not on a piece of paper?" Bella asked again.

"Then we can add another piece of paper," Joseph replied.

We both sat back on the sofa and allowed the kids to all step in and write their names on the papers. Some of the younger ones simply began to draw on the surplus paper.

The obvious candidates became clear, although there were a few surprises.

Bella had taken a piece of paper and scribbled 'Doctor' on it with her name below. I looked at Joseph with a surprised look on my face. "Very nice Bella," he said with encouragement, and I could tell she was pleased.

At the end of the exercise, it became clear that there were still many jobs that were unaccounted for. No one had really volunteered for gardening. I held up the paper, and Luna, who was a year younger than her sister Bella, volunteered.

"Why aren't *your* names written?" Daniel asked.

I didn't know how to answer this, and Joseph understood when he looked at me, "we are going to help out wherever we can." Daniel and the rest of the kids seemed satisfied with this.

"What about the exodus?" Daniel asked.

"What about it?" Joseph asked.

"How will we defend ourselves?" Daniel continued.

"So, defense?" I said. I took a piece of paper and wrote, 'Defense.' I could hear Joseph in my head saying, without actually saying it, 'we are a peaceful people.' "Maybe, we can do things like, build a lookout," I said.

"Or alert the compound when people are in the area," Daniel exclaimed excitedly.

"Yes, non-violent things," I said trying to appease Joseph while recognizing the impending threat that was looming on all sides.

Daniel took the paper from my hand and excitedly wrote down his name on the paper.

"But you already wrote it on Construction," Joseph said.

"Hey, you said we could write our name on many pieces of paper," Daniel complained.

Joseph smiled, "yes, I did," realizing that his words had come back to bite him.

Joseph and I exited the compound. We looked around and walked up above the compound near the observation deck, but without standing on the deck itself. We both sat with our backs against a log. And I found myself looking around at the slightest sound, more aware of what was happening in the woods around us.

"The real test is if they do something about what they volunteered for," Joseph said under his breath.

"I agree," I said. "The challenge will how they get these skills. We're just kids."

"Just kids, but look at how far we've come," Joseph corrected me. "Violet is feeding all of us, rationing meals into portions. It can't be easy," he said. "She works at it tirelessly. And no one really helps her. She's in that kitchen all day long. We just all show up, and there's food. Hardly any of us say thanks." I nodded silently, allowing him an opportunity to vent. I had struck a chord. "She keeps it all organized too, all the pots and pans," he said before stopping and staring blankly in the direction of the lake.

I pushed aside some decaying leaves with my shoe, revealing the rich, black earth, beneath them. I flicked my eyes up toward him and then back toward the ground wondering what he was thinking about. Probably what I was thinking about: how much I had taken my own parents for granted. They did everything for me, and I hardly said thanks.

"We should go to a library," I said, trying to break the impasse. "A library?"

"Yeah. There has gotta be one in the smaller towns nearby. We don't even have to go to Burlington." I could see he was thinking for a bit, but I continued. "We could get books on various subjects, good books. For Violet, we could pick up some cookbooks, and for Madison, we could get a book on identifying fish."

"Do you think a small library would have all of that?" Joseph said.

He was right. We kept going to smaller places and selling ourselves short. "I don't," I said to be honest, "but it's the safest option right now."

"Alrighty then, we leave tonight," he said, brightening up once again. But as he stood, he stopped in his place.

I arose from my seated position and looked in the direction he was looking. At the mouth of the lake were several kids. I instinctively grabbed him and pulled him along with me back to the ground.

"They most likely can't see us," he said.

"Sorry," I replied, and he responded with one of his grins. We kept low and entered the compound through the glass enclosure.

We didn't let on about the others and Joseph reminded everyone to stay inside.

"How am I going to grow plants?" Luna asked, "there is no sunlight in here!" She was right. Of course, we hadn't told her or anyone else about what was in the terrarium.

"Let us think," Joseph said, as he guided me to the office with his hand on my lower back. He closed the door and sat on the floor behind the desk with his legs crossed and his hands in his lap. I sat beside him with my knees up to my chest and my arms wrapped around them and just looked at him.

"Maybe we're doing this all wrong," he finally said. I just stayed silent. "You and I are always being looked to for guidance, we are always making the decisions. I mean, Luna for instance, is coming to us to ask where to plant the garden. The whole point of the exercise was so that they would handle this." He was getting a little animated and rightfully so because that *was* the point of the exercise.

"I agree with you," I said. "But like I said, we are just kids." He nodded.

"We will always have to help them," he said. "We have to divide our responsibilities. I can help Luna with the gardening, Brad with the animal husbandry, just as an example. You could help Daniel with construction and with defense."

"But then we would be apart," I said. He looked at me, reassuringly and took my left hand from its position around my knee and clasped it within the two of his.

"We will *never* be apart," he said. I felt a warmth inside of me, and I nodded. "Besides, I am not letting you out of my sight," he said laughing.

I laughed.

"Inside the compound, we work separately, but when we go outside, we need to be together," he said. "If something happens to you," he said before trailing off. I watched his smile turn to a somber expression.

I allowed my legs to fall outstretched and pulled his head into my chest with both arms and held him.

"I love you too," I said.

He pulled up and looked at my face, "what?" he asked calmly. "I love you," I repeated.

He grabbed me and held me tightly in his arms. It took me this long to say the words, but it was what Brad had told me the first few nights he met us. He saw what neither of us could say. *Love*.

CHAPTER

Fourteen

WE DECIDED BRAD WOULD stay behind at the compound with the others. As the eldest, he would be in charge while both Joseph and I were away. We had been studying the map, but it was too large an area to depict libraries.

"Schools," Brad said.

"Schools?" I repeated.

"Yes, schools have libraries."

"This is another one of your strengths Brad," I said to him in a serious voice. He smiled. I was realizing that giving praise where due was empowering.

"But I don't know where the nearest school is, except Milton and Burlington," he said. At these words, my heart sunk.

"And, I guess it would have to be a high school," I said, "because the only books we get in our school are kids' books." This is something that none of us had thought of until then.

"There are schools also here," Brad said, refocusing on the map.

"Acton?" I asked.

"Yes," he replied.

"But it looks far," Joseph said.

"It's a smaller town though," Brad answered.

"So safer," I said.

"Okay," Joseph said decisively, "we will drive to Acton."

When night fell, we left the compound. The moon was invisible, probably the end of the lunar cycle, making it pitch black outside. The stars overhead did little to improve our visibility and we could barely see in front of us. We had our flashlights, but we couldn't use them, not without possibly alerting others to our presence.

We walked south along Guelph Line, sticking to grassy areas of the road to dampen the sound of our footsteps. In the distance, we could hear voices, and any time we heard a twig snap or sound, we knelt and took a moment to peer into the darkness. An impossibility of sorts. Someone could be standing a few meters from us, and we wouldn't know.

It was about five minutes before we reached the car, and it looked undisturbed. We took the branches off and I unlocked the doors. We quickly got in, started the car, and began to drive north on Guelph Line. We dared not turn on any lights, to look at the map, until we were well north of the compound.

As we drove, Joseph directed me down various sideroads winding north-eastward.

"There's not much to this place, is there?" I asked Joseph as we drove into Acton, which was positioned at the intersection of two major roads.

"Definitely not, but that's a good thing. Pull over here," he said pointing to a gas station on the right. "Wait here and keep the car running." I had no intention of turning off the vehicle.

The front door of the station and most of the windows were shattered. The car headlights illuminated the interior, which was ransacked with few items remaining on the shelves. I watched the area around us for any signs of movement or people, but there was nothing. The near complete darkness beyond the headlights had me on edge.

Moments later, he came out with some maps. "I got these," he said putting the maps on his lap as he entered the car. "Drive! Let's get out of town, as quickly as possible," he said, not needing to tell me, and I did, driving away quickly.

When we reached the eastward edge of town, we pulled off a small road on the right. We rolled down the windows and listened. It was dead quiet. We decided it was safe to turn on the interior lights and we looked at the map.

"Great, it has symbols," he said with excitement. "There is actually a high school and a library," he said looking up at me. "Which one do we go to first?"

"Well, which one is closer?"

"The high school."

"Lead the way," I said as I turned off the interior light and turned the vehicle.

He directed me through subdivisions, along lifeless streets, until we reached the school, where I turned into the empty parking lot and stopped.

The school itself was rather large, two stories and similar in size to our school in Toronto. It surprised me for a such a small town, but I surmised that students from nearby towns were probably bused in.

I had never been on a school bus. I imagined it was like something I had seen in movies. A bunch of unruly kids screaming and throwing crap at each other – no thanks. I usually walked or took the city bus if the weather was poor, but often for the latter, I simply stayed at home. My mother didn't mind, and my father wasn't around enough.

The orange-colored brick stood out in the darkness. The roof looked a metallic brown, but it was difficult to tell. There were two sets of orange doors near the front of the school.

"It would be a good place for people to stay," I said.

"Yes, it would," Joseph answered in agreement.

"I am worried people *are* in there. And if not in there, certainly anyone in these houses could be watching us," I said pointing toward the unlit houses, whose shapes appeared darker than the darkness itself. "I don't feel comfortable here."

"Then let's go," he said.

We drove out of the school parking lot, along Cedar Road and north on Churchill Road taking a left on McDonald Boulevard.

The name 'McDonald' had me thinking of the restaurant. "I am craving a cheeseburger right now," I told him.

"A cheeseburger?"

"Yes, McDonald, as in McDonald's." He laughed.

"My mom never let me eat there. It was always homecooked food." We turned left on Wallace Street.

"We are lucky you thought to get that map. The place looks small, but we would never have found anything here, especially in the dark." We then turned left on Main Street North and then left on School Lane.

We pulled into the library parking lot and stopped in front of the doors, which were intact.

"There are no houses around here," Joseph said, "that's good."

"There is a school over there though," I said dismayed, pointing to the left. Its white front was more visible in the darkness.

"I guess that's why it's called School Lane," Joseph responded. A detail that neither of us had picked up on.

We stopped the car, waited a moment to see if there was any movement, and when we were certain there wasn't, we exited the vehicle.

The front of the library was made of grey and brown stone. A large metallic structure stood beside and atop the main doors. The doors were locked, and no one had broken in.

Joseph went to take a stone from the grassy area to the right of the doors. Instead of throwing it through the front doors, he threw it through the first of the three windows that were beside the door. The glass shattered and fell to the ground.

"We should be okay," he said, helping me climb inside.

We turned on our flashlights but kept them pointed downwards to limit them being visible through the windows and doors. Joseph picked up a few bags near the front desk, although it took a few minutes to find them. I had started to walk down the aisles of the library.

"This is going to take a while," I called out to Joseph.

"We have time," he replied calmly.

I found perusing the books relaxing. We were always in and out of places, trying to hurry and in the dark, in an unfamiliar place, with so many book titles to read, this would not be an in-and-out job. We needed to take our time.

I peered over at Joseph from time to time. He was walking along the fiction aisles, but I wasn't sure why. Nothing over there would be of any use to us, but I let him be. I, on the other hand, had already filled about five bags in about the span of ten minutes. Anything at all that was interesting and sounded remotely educational, I just threw in. Edible Wild Plants, Clinical Microbiology, Pharmaceutical Dictionary, Five Ingredients or Less Cookbook, Arithmetic for Grade Two, to name a few.

When we were done, we had about twenty bags full, although I had done most of the picking. Joseph stood outside the window, and I handed him each bag. We then loaded them into the trunk of the car and began the trip back to the compound. We had made it in and out of Acton with no issues, no roadblocks, indeed, the town was seemingly deserted.

As we drove south along Guelph Line, we could see fires in the distance, some closer to the road. Their embers floated up slowly into the night sky. Around the fires moved shadowy figures, some, almost dance-like.

"How could it be safe for them to light fires?" I asked nudging my head in the direction of the fields.

"Maybe it's not as dangerous as we think. Maybe it's just people like us fleeing the cities, maybe that's where the real danger lies."

"Maybe," I said flatly. I wasn't convinced. We had seen enough to know that there were real dangers out there.

We parked the car near where we started and covered it with some brush. We couldn't carry all the bags between us and decided we would come back another night for more – the only option without drawing unwanted attention.

We were startled by the sound of twigs snapping and voices. I turned on the flashlight and cast its glare on the surrounding forest. A boy and girl emerged and walked cautiously toward us.

The boy looked slightly older than the girl but was gaunt and undernourished. Both had fair blonde hair, slightly soiled with dirt and unkempt. Their faces were somewhat clean, but I could tell they were crudely washed, and the runs of water cut clear paths through layers of dirt.

"We mean you no harm," the boy said immediately.

"We don't either," Joseph replied putting down the bags he was carrying.

"Are there others?" I asked doing the same.

"No," the girl said after a short pause, "we haven't seen anyone around. We were close by when we heard your car."

"My name is Anders, and this is my sister Freya. I'm eleven and she's ten," he said.

Joseph looked at me and I nodded my head slightly, having not felt the least bit threatened. "Are you hungry?" Joseph asked.

"Very much so," Anders replied, almost with an edge of desperation in his voice. I opened the trunk to the car once again.

"Can you carry a couple of bags of books each?" I asked. The boy looked puzzled.

"We have a place, we have food," Joseph said, "you can stay with us. You both seem innocent enough."

They eagerly grabbed two bags each and followed us to the compound.

"What is this place?" Freya asked as the compound came into view.

"It's our home," I said.

"It's your home now too, if you want it to be," Joseph continued. When we got inside, everyone was sleeping, and we tried our best to be quiet.

"There are so many of you and you have power!" Anders said excitedly in a low voice.

"Please take a seat somewhere and I will get you some food. You can leave the bags anywhere," Joseph said. I sat beside them both and moments later, Joseph arrived and sat with us, handing each of us some food and something to drink.

"Thank-you," Freya said, although she was already eating when she said it.

"Where are you from?" I asked them.

"We are from Waterdown," Anders responded.

"Where's that?" Joseph asked. This clearly puzzled our guests.

"My dad built this compound," I said, which wasn't entirely true, at least to my knowledge.

"We are from Toronto," Joseph continued. Our two guests looked interested.

"Did you travel far?" I asked them.

"Yes, sorry, we walked from Waterdown, away from the city, from Burlington," Freya said chiming in. "Things are bad there."

Anders continued, "there are gangs."

"We have heard about the gangs and seen them from a distance," Joseph said.

"They are *very* violent," Freya said.

"They captured us," Anders continued. "They wanted us to work for them, they threatened us." Joseph looked at me.

"But we escaped," Freya said interrupting him.

After they had finished eating, we let them shower and showed them a place where they could sleep.

"Stay inside, it's not safe out there," I said. The irony of what I was telling them. They had traveled through the worst of it, they knew more than we did, and yet I was telling them to stay inside and to be safe. I awoke Brad briefly and told him of our guests, since he was an early riser, and I didn't want him or anyone else to be frightened by their presence. I didn't know if he understood though and he simply mumbled something before falling back asleep. Joseph and I then retired to our place under the desk in the office.

When the morning came, Joseph had already awakened leaving me by myself in our cubby hole. When I entered the living room, he looked in my direction. Brad was sitting next to him and moved aside, patting the seat. "Funny," I said in a sarcastic voice. Joseph then did the same and his grin widened on his face. I walked over and slumped myself dramatically between them.

Anders and Freya were both eating copious amounts of food, attentively listening to Brad who was rambling on about the city and the rabbits that he caught. Joseph yawned and put his head on my shoulder, he was bored. He could tell I was about to say something and put some food in my mouth to shut me up. I could take a hint. He put some more in when he heard me finish swallowing it.

Joseph pecked a kiss on my cheek, leaned back in the sofa and put his arm behind me. Anders and Freya look at each other. "They are a couple," Brad said pointing to us with a grin, "but I'm single," he said looking at Freya.

At this I stood up. There would be no way to keep me quiet any longer I thought, and I didn't want to disappoint Joseph. "We should get the rest of those books," I said.

"You should sleep some more," Joseph said, "the books can wait."

"I'm okay," I responded and put on my shoes coaxing Joseph away from our newest members. 'Members' I thought, like all of this was becoming a club. I opened the front door and Joseph pulled me back just when a sharpened stick struck the frame.

"We're in trouble," Joseph said closing the door immediately.

CHAPTER

Fifteen

E VERYONE WITH THE AWARENESS to understand looked in our direction. Some of the younger kids just kept playing like nothing had happened.

"I think we have company," Joseph said, "and they are hostile."

"They just threw a spear at our heads," I said cynically, the adrenaline wearing off a bit.

"Mia, take the kids into the enclosure," Joseph said, "we don't want to scare them."

Moments later, there was thumping against the metal door.

"They can't get in, can they?" Freya asked.

"No, the door is like a tank," Joseph said. "We need to see what is going on out there."

"The second exit," I said. "We need to go up top and we need to see what we are up against."

"Who will go?" Brad asked.

"I will," Daniel said.

"I think you'd better sit this one out," Joseph said to him, trying hard to not hurt his feelings.

"But I am in charge of defense," Daniel whined.

"Yes, you are," Joseph began.

"And besides, I am small, and I can sneak around," Daniel continued cutting Joseph off.

At this, I just nodded to Joseph, and we went into the enclosure and stood beneath the second exit.

"Wait," I said. I came back with some brown pants and a green sweater. "Wear these," I said to Daniel. "It will help you blend in with the surroundings."

"Good idea," Joseph said. "Daniel, we need to know how many there are, where they are positioned, and if you can hear anything, what they are planning," Joseph said. Daniel nodded. "Good luck," he said tapping Daniel on the shoulder before he scaled the ladder and exited. "Now we wait," Joseph said.

About ten minutes passed, and then fifteen. We were getting worried.

"Something's wrong," Brad said pacing back and forth, "I can feel it." He was making me nervous.

A minute later, Violet came into the glass enclosure, Brad was right, something was wrong. "Andrew, there is a knock at the door," she said. We all rushed through to the entrance. Before I could speak, there was a bang on the door. A muffled voice on the other side said, "we have the boy."

"Unless Daniel has told them something, they have no idea who we are if we don't speak with them," Joseph whispered.

"One of us needs to go out the exit," I said.

"You are not going anywhere without me," Joseph said firmly.

"We don't even know if they are at the exit, waiting for us," Brad said.

"We know, because if they knew where that exit was, they would be coming in here," Joseph said.

"Okay, so what do we do?" I asked turning my attention back to Joseph.

"We go together," he said looking at me.

"I can go," Brad said.

"No," I said shaking my head. I was thinking that Brad barely sensed us on the day that we met him, now he expects to covertly figure out what is going on out there?

"I have a plan," Joseph said.

"Do you have guns I don't know about?" I asked.

"We don't need guns or weapons, we have each other, and we are smarter than any adversary," he responded.

"It's because of us," Freya interrupted.

"Freya," Anders pleaded in protest.

"What is it that you're not telling us?" I asked as we all turned toward her.

"It's the gang, we were in the gang, I mean it has to be," she blurted out.

"What gang?" Joseph asked.

Freya sat down and glanced at Anders who nodded at her. "So, I was his girlfriend, the leader of the gang, I mean, but we ran away," she continued.

"And now he wants you back," Brad exclaimed in frustration. "I am definitely going!" Brad said starting to climb the ladder. "I gotta save my girl."

"Please," I pleaded, agitated at Brads dramatics, "we need a plan that is far better than you trying to go gung-ho just to impress Freya here." Brad blushed.

"Freya, please continue," I said.

"He broke into our house one night, and had told us that we either join his gang or die,"

"We had no choice really," Anders interjected.

"So, we did, and not long after that he started coming onto me and telling me that I was his. Like his possession or something. He started keeping me from my brother. He would send him out on raids, and I would have to stay home. Days were passing where I wouldn't see Anders. Then, one night, we escaped. We just ran as fast as we could into the woods and hid, and when they stopped looking for us, we kept walking to here." She stared at the floor, and I looked around at the room at the others. They seemed to believe her story, but something didn't make sense.

"But if you lost them, how did they find you?" I interjected. Both Anders and Freya looked at each other in a way that made me uneasy. They were being untruthful.

"Listen, if there's something you're not telling us, you need to start," I began to yell. "There's no way, that they followed you from Waterdown, all the way here, over days of walking." But the two remained silent.

"Andrew, there's no reason to yell at her," Brad exclaimed.

"Daniel is out there," I said calmly but angrily, "and I am going to get him back and then I want the truth. I want to know what we are up against." I looked at Anders and Freya and could tell they understood.

"One of them followed us in a car. Our job was to find places to infiltrate and pillage. This time they let me come along," Freya said, "they felt me being a girl would make it easier." They could see the anger on my face. "But once I was with my brother, and out of ear shot, we just wanted to get away, and when we met you, we didn't know what to say or do. We hoped they wouldn't come."

I began to climb, "Andrew, where are you going?" Joseph asked.

"I'm going to have a look around and see what we are up against," and then I looked squarely at Freya and her brother, "and to deal with it."

I pushed open the hatch just barely and began to look around. It was difficult since the hatch lay in a depression within the rock. I listened. I could hear some voices, but they were in the distance and there were no sounds nearby except some birds. I waited a few minutes before opening the hatch all the way and sticking my head out. I looked along the boardwalk, through the forest, and up into the trees. "There's nothing," I whispered to Joseph who was below me.

We exited the hatch and covered it. We retreated deeper into the forest, away from the boardwalk where we could be seen, northward, away from the compound and parking lot.

"Where are we going?" Joseph asked.

"Trust me," I said, taking his hand.

We kept low, and walked for at least a few minutes until the compound, lake and boardwalk were out of sight. We then turned westward toward the compound road. Along the way, I picked up some evergreen branches. I looked at Joseph and smirked, "I am taking some pointers from you," I said handing him a couple of evergreen branches.

We obscured ourselves with the branches while continuing to walk. I then led us back toward the parking lot. "We are circling around," I told Joseph. When we neared the parking lot, we stayed deep within the tree line behind some bushes.

"Keep an eye out," I said to Joseph before he responded, "I have a smart boyfriend." Boyfriend, I thought. Another word. I wondered if he were taking pointers from Brad who had just referred to Freya as his girlfriend.

There were several people in the parking lot, four boys and one girl. All of them were around our age and all of them had weapons. It didn't look like there were any guns, but they all had spears and one had a machete. Then I saw Daniel.

"I'm going to kill them," I said under my breath. Daniel was kneeling beside the girl and his face was covered in blood. Joseph picked up on my anger, cautioning me against doing anything rash. "Let's go back," I whispered as we headed back in the direction we came, mindful that there may be others.

The noise of us entering frightened everyone. "It's just us," I said as we climbed down the ladder.

"I'm glad you guys came back, we were getting worried, a few more minutes and I was about to go commando," Brad said. I turned my head and rolled my eyes.

"We need to keep a cool head," Joseph said.

Casting aside questions from everyone. I explained what we had seen, and Freya and Anders described each of the gang members as they realized who we were talking about.

"We only need to go after one," Joseph said, "your boyfriend," he continued, looking at Freya.

"Me?" Brad asked.

"No, not you," several of us said together. I felt a certain satisfaction that it wasn't only me who was annoyed at Brad's obsessive behavior.

"You said that he wants you," I said looking at Freya pausing to see if there was any reaction – there wasn't. "And he's obviously not someone we can take in, not after what he did to Daniel. And, right now, I don't believe that even if we did give him what he wants that he would release him." Brad perked up at this.

"If we got rid of him, would the others back down?" I asked them both. I was surprised that even Joseph never made a comment on my insinuation that we should kill the leader.

"If you go out there and attack them, they' just kill Daniel," Anders responded.

"I wasn't thinking of going out there," I responded to him as I nudged my head in Freya's direction.

"You're not sending *her* out there?" Brad asked inquisitively.

"If he really does want her, she'll come to no harm, and he's not going to expect what he has got coming to him," I said flatly. I left the group and went to the lab and grabbed a needle. Then I went into the kitchen and filled the needle with Bleach, before returning to the others.

"I want you to go out there. I want you to say that you are sorry for running away and that both of you want to come back. Then I want you to hug him, and I want you to inject him in the chest with this as he embraces you." I handed her the needle. "It's Bleach," I said firmly.

There was a silence that descended on the room, and I could tell that everyone, including Joseph, was shocked at my plan.

"You want me to kill him?" Freya asked quietly.

"He's going to kill Daniel," I said, "he's going to perhaps punish you and your brother for leaving, and one of us could get hurt as well."

"What happens then?" Brad asked.

"We exit together, all of us older kids, taking whatever tools we can use as weapons," Joseph chimed in.

"We show them that we don't leave our own to die," Mia said.

"That this is *our* place!" Violet screamed.

The older of us stood near the door opening, Freya, Anders, Joseph, Brad, Violet, Mia, and I, each holding a makeshift weapon of choice, a needle, a baseball bat, which Joseph held for Anders, a hammer, metal bar, a meat cleaver, a couple of shovels.

I pressed the hand symbol and the door opened and Freya walked out while the rest of us stayed hidden around the corner.

She began to cry with such persuasiveness that it left even me doubtful that she was faking. "I am sorry," she said walking toward him, "we shouldn't have left."

"Where's your brother?" A boy's voice boomed.

"I'm here," Anders said stepping out slightly behind her.

"I'm sorry," Freya wept again, wiping away her tears.

I peered around the edge of the wall as she embraced him. She held him tightly, but he was distracted by Anders.

"We want to come home," Anders said.

"What the?" the boy said in disbelief as Freya stepped back.

"I'm sorry," Freya said shaking with her hands over her mouth, "I'm so sorry," crying even more, and at this I was sure she was not faking.

Anders then reached for her and pulled her back further. "Are you okay?" the other girl asked as the boy pulled the empty needle from his chest before collapsing on the ground.

The lot of us then ran out screaming at the group with our weapons in the air before attacking them. It was over quickly, as the group disbanded, leaving Daniel. The boy lay on the ground holding his chest and convulsing. We kept away from him and waited until it was over. Anders held Freya while she wept.

After a few minutes later, Brad broke the silence, "What do we do with him?" I began to pick up his arms and drag him, and Brad helped. We dragged him into the tree line away from the compound. The others watched. "We're just going to leave him here?" Brad asked.

"Yes," I responded, "let the animals have him." We then went into the compound with the others.

It was a somber evening. Except for the younger of us who didn't witness the day's events, we sat around, quiet, our moods dampened. Mia was content to have Daniel back and kept him close. He was a little despondent and I worried that the ordeal had scarred him. I was always hard on him, and I would have to remind myself to be kinder.

She and Bella had cleaned his wounds. Luckily much of the blood had flowed from a single cut on his forehead, which should have required stitches.

Freya was greatly affected by what she had done. She took a life today. A necessity, I reasoned, but a difficult one. I stood up from the couch and walked through to the office and sat in my father's chair. I lay my head back and swayed slightly from side to side until my eyes drew heavy and I drifted asleep.

CHAPTER

Sixteen

Y OU LOOK LIKE YOU have a cold," Joseph said to Freya over breakfast. Violet had made pancakes, but since we never had any eggs or milk, they turned out flat. I sat begrudgingly eating them, dipping them into the maple syrup she had rationed each of us. It did little to improve the taste. This was another item that we could make if we had to, I thought, but we'd have to wait until the winter and learn how to tap a maple tree.

"Yeah, my nose is all stuffy, and I'm feeling, overall, pretty crappy," Freya replied.

"I feel fine," Brad said as he stuffed another forkful in his mouth. Unlike the rest of us, he looked like he was enjoying them. I hadn't forgiven Freya and Anders yet, allowing Joseph to converse with them this morning. I didn't trust them.

"You can stay in an office," Joseph said, "isolate yourself a little and I will have Mia bring you a blanket and Violet make you some soup."

"Thank-you," Freya said as she left the living room and walked through to the office.

"I hope the rest of us don't get it," Brad said.

"Isn't she your *girlfriend*?" Daniel mocked. "Ha-ha, you missed me," he yelled leaping from the couch, avoiding a close swat from Brad's hand.

I stood up from my seat leaving my plate of half-finished pancakes. I could see everyone was returning to their normal except me. I had slept really well, too well. It bothered me that I never had so much as a nightmare. Yeah, Freya was the one who put the needle in the gang boss's chest, but it was me who told her to do it and I felt so little remorse.

I began walking toward the front entrance which caught the attention of Joseph. "Where are you going?" he asked running up behind me gently grabbing my arm. I sighed. "Are you okay?" he asked. I could hear the concern in his voice. I wasn't, I needed to get away from all the banter and focus on doing something, but I lied and nodded my head.

"I figured I'd go try to find a place to dig a garden," I said after a few seconds' silence.

"But it's not safe outside," he replied. I wondered if my father had wanted us to stay cooped up in here forever. He must have known that our supplies would run low, that we would need to loot for food. That all the surviving kids would have devolved in the absence of adults, sitting around campfires plotting attacks instead of singing Kumbaya.

"I have to do something, I can't stay in here forever," I said, "we can't pretend that all this isn't happening." I could see that, once again, I saddened him. I kept hurting him and I hated myself for it.

"Okay, let's go out," he said in a buoyant voice putting on his sneakers.

I was less careful exiting the compound than before, but that's perhaps because I knew Joseph was on the lookout. We walked slowly up the embankment, me taking time to cover the entrance of the path by pushing leaves and twigs over what was already becoming a well-worn trail.

Joseph held my hand, entwining his fingers within my own, and we walked north on the boardwalk.

"I don't trust Anders and Freya," I blurted out, "they lied to us." I could feel Joseph contemplating his response.

"She wouldn't have done what she did yesterday, if they weren't with *us*," he said.

I nodded, "yeah, I know. I just want it to be *us*, only us," I said turning to him and stopping. "I don't want to be forced to take in everyone who might not look like a threat, never really knowing. I mean we lucked out with *Brad*," I said.

"Braaad," Joseph wailed sticking out his tongue and shaking his head from side to side.

I laughed. "Well, I know he drives me crazy, but he's a good guy."

"He drives you crazy?" Joseph joked sarcastically.

"Stop," I said laughing under my breath.

The boardwalk ended when we reached the old Crawford family home. The house had burned down and all that remained was the foundation. Beside the house was a small meadow where I led Joseph and we stood in the warmth of the sun.

"This would be a good place for a garden," I said kicking the earth with the toe of my shoe, "we could dig here without hitting too much limestone."

"What about the terrarium?" Joseph asked. I sat down on the grass, still grasping his hand, pulling him down beside me.

"You and I have been the only ones in there," I said. I paused a moment, "it's our place." I could see him smile slightly as I scratched the soil with a small stick, I had found beside me. "It's just, I don't even understand why it's there, and I want time to explore it."

"You don't want anyone to spoil it," he said.

"Yeah," I said nodding my head.

"I get that," he said nodding. "So yeah, this looks like a great place for a garden," he said looking around smiling.

I perked up. "What is it?" Joseph asked.

I shook my head, "I thought I heard my name."

"Wait," he said. This time it was louder.

"Andrew!" I could hear Violet screaming from the compound. She had reached the age in her life where her voice was breaking and teetered between a full-bodied voice and a shrill one. Her shrieks sent shivers down my spine.

I grabbed Joseph by the hand, and we began to run in the direction of the compound. I had to pace myself so that Joseph could keep up. After everything that happened yesterday, the last thing we needed was Violet screaming.

"What is it?" I hollered when I saw her.

"Andrew, Joseph, you have to come quick, it's Freya."

"What's wrong?" I asked her as we closed in.

"There's blood," Violet continued. I couldn't tell if she was out of breath or simply panicking or both. "She's coughing up a lot of blood."

"Let's go," Joseph said. The three of us ran as quickly as we could back to the compound.

There are no words I could use to describe what we walked into. Many of the kids had gone into the glass enclosure, leaving Freya, Anders, and Brad in the middle of the living area. Freya was lying on her side and the hands of Anders and Brad were covered with blood.

"Get away from her," Joseph said commandingly.

"But she's my sister," Anders protested.

"She has the virus," Joseph continued, "can't you see? Why else would she be coughing up blood?"

At this Freya, pushed Anders back with her hand. He had been sitting behind her. "Go," she whispered. Anders stood up along with Brad who had already taken a few steps back.

"Go shower now," I yelled at them, "and don't touch anything!"

Both Joseph and I kept our distance from Freya.

I could hear the showers running in the bathroom and Anders sobbing with the occasional boom of Brads low voice echoing, I assumed to comfort him, but it was impossible to make out what he was saying.

"There's nothing you can do, is there?" Freya whispered as she coughed. Joseph just shook his head. "I deserve this, for what I did yesterday," she whispered continuing to cough up blood, which she spat on the floor.

"You don't deserve this," I said under my breath, unsure if she heard me from my seat on the floor across the corridor. I felt even more responsible now. I had acted too hastily, there might have been other options.

Moments later the shower stopped, and Brad and Anders exited the washroom wrapped in towels. I was surprised at how quickly they showered, but I ignored them.

"Brad, take him into the office and stay in there," Joseph ordered upon seeing them.

"I want to see my sister," Anders said yelling.

I shook my head with such subtle movement, but Brad understood and literally picked him up, taking him into the office. I could hear some yelling and then sobbing.

As the hour passed, we watched as Freya drift out of consciousness and then she stopped breathing. I wiped the tears from my eyes. It was reminiscent of my father passing. I wish I never yelled at her, but it was too late.

We put on some gloves we found in the kitchen and wrapped her in a sheet. We then walked her out the front door, up the embankment and along the boardwalk to the meadow. I dug a hole and placed her body inside and Joseph covered her with soil. I made a makeshift cross out of two sticks and stuck it in the ground. We sat there for a moment. We had buried one of our own, she *was* one of our own.

I could tell that Joseph was affected by this more than I. I put my arm around him for a moment and he rested his head on my shoulder and began to cry. It wasn't just about losing Freya. It wasn't about losing relatives or our parents even. We were thrust into a terrifying new world where we had to assume responsibilities that we weren't prepared for. Here we were having to burry our dead at eleven years old.

When we came back to the compound, everyone was still where we left them. The floor was covered with blood, and Joseph and I spent the next hour cleaning it with bleach.

We threw away our gloves and continued wiping all surfaces of the compound. We avoided the office and the glass enclosure.

We opened the front door and allowed the air to circulate, to rid the place of fumes, which were making me rather light-headed. We did most of this silently. Neither Joseph nor I said anything to each other. We knew what had to be done, and we did it.

"Where are your clothes?" I asked Brad as I went to the office. Both were still wrapped in towels.

"In the washroom," Brad said still holding Anders.

I wondered if Anders knew whether his sister had died yet, whether he understood why we were wearing gloves, why we had left the living room. We took the clothes from the washroom and put them in a bag.

"We will burn these tonight," I said to Joseph, and he nodded. We had a few good months, free of death, free of the virus, and now it had come once again knocking on our door.

Joseph and I sat in the living room. He reached across the sofa and held my hand. I needed this, but I felt he did more. I held it tightly.

The door to the glass enclosure opened. "Go back inside!" Joseph shouted. I had never heard him like that before. I took my other hand and put it on his and looked at him.

"I'm thinking about my mom," he said as tears welled within his eyes. I pulled him close and for the next little while I just allowed him to cry until he fell asleep. He showed such strength all the time and to see him vulnerable, deepened my compassion for him. I took a blanket and covered him, stood up, and did what had to be done.

I went to the office and knocked gently on the door.

"Come in," Brad said so quietly that his low booming voice was almost unrecognizable. "He's sleeping," he said pointing to Anders.

"How do you feel?"

"I'm alright," he responded. I nodded my head to the side to have him come out of the office and we stood in the hallway.

"Joseph is sleeping too," I said motioning my head back to the sofa where he was lying. "How is this possible?"

"I dunno."

"Do you think it is starting again?"

"I dunno." I was about to get upset but realized that it would be unfair. Neither of us knew why Freya had come down with the virus.

"We need to wake him," I said to Brad while lifting my hand slightly in the direction of Anders. "You should get dressed," which was my cue for him to leave the room.

"Anders," I said gently touching his upper arm. He was lying on his side. He opened his eyes and sat up.

"My sister?" he asked.

I shook my head, and he began to cry as he sat up with his knees toward his chest and his hands on his face. I reached out and touched his shoulder and left my hand upon it, "I'm sorry," I said.

"Can I see her?" he asked. I shook my head.

"I want to see her!" he said angrily standing up and knocking me out of the way, however, Brad had returned to the office.

"She's gone," Brad said, holding Anders back as he tried to leave. "Let her go," he said repeatedly.

Eventually Anders gave up trying to fight with Brad, fell to the floor and began to cry once again. I crawled across the floor and held him. After his crying abated somewhat, I looked him in the face and asked him the question that I needed answered, "do you know how she got sick?" Anders shook his head without speaking.

"Some kids die from the virus," Brad said, "remember my sister?" I remembered, because it also happened to two of my nieces, but that was at the beginning of the outbreak, we were well beyond that now. I wondered if the virus was still circulating, but then where did she get it?

"It's been several months now," I said to Brad.

"Maybe they didn't get exposed," he responded.

"What do you mean I asked? Is that possible?"

"I dunno," he responded once again.

It was irritating me that he raised, what seemed like a plausible explanation but had no answer.

"Anders, I am sorry, but we need to find out what happened, otherwise, all of us could be at risk," I said as he looked up at me. His eyes were emotionless and although I felt bad for pressuring him, I needed answers.

"Is Joseph still sleeping?" I asked Brad.

Brad looked down the hallway, "yup. Want me to wake him?"

"Of course not," I snapped. "Sorry," I continued, shaking my head realizing that I hurt his feelings. Joseph was better at handling this type of situation, he had a way of gradually guiding people along, whereas I just wanted to get answers immediately.

"We didn't get sick," Anders said.

"What do you mean?" I asked him, but he didn't continue.

Brad sat down beside us. He had one knee up to his chest and the other folded under him. He put one hand on the floor and one on the shoulder of Anders.

"You never got sick?" he asked Anders in disbelief, who simply shook his head in response. "Everyone gets sick," Brad said. "You got sick, right Andrew?" He said looking at me.

"Yes," I said.

"But you recovered. I got sick and I recovered, Anders is saying they never caught the virus."

"Is this right?" I asked Anders and he nodded his head.

"We have another problem," Brad said.

"What's that?" I looked at him even more concerned since I think I knew what he was going to say.

"We can get the virus again and again, we could all get sick again," and at these words I let go of Anders and sat against the door in panic. He was right. I had heard it on the news. After a while, we lost immunity and could get re-infected.

"They injected us with something as well," Anders said solemnly.

"What do you mean?" I asked puzzled.

"They injected us and sent us here, they injected us," he said repeating it over and over, sobbing. Neither Brad nor I could get him to say another word.

Within hours, Anders was sick. He had a fever, he was coughing, and sweating. Both Brad and I left him in the office with some water and closed the door. I was getting a headache.

I sat in the living room with Joseph who was now awake, and we had decided to bring everyone in again from the glass enclosure.

"Where is Anders and Freya?" Mia was the first to ask.

"Anders is sick, he is in the office, no one is to go in there – absolutely no one," I said flatly. "Freya, died," I continued.

Several of the kids began to cry and others looked visibly alarmed.

"We're going to be okay," Joseph said in his calm voice. I was glad that he thought so, I certainly needed to hear it. He looked at me. "Does anyone else feel sick?" No one raised their hands. "That's good," he said. "We're going to have to go to get some medical supplies," he said, "we have nothing here. Brad, you're in charge."

The glass door of the pharmacy had been shattered. Shards of glass were scattered on the inside and outside of the doorway. Although the door was protected with iron bars, they were not narrow enough to prevent the hands of a child from gaining access to the lock.

I slowly pulled open the door and tried to avoid stepping on the glass, instructing the others to do the same. We entered cautiously, although I was relatively confident no others were inside.

Each of us grabbed one of the black plastic grocery baskets that were at the front. Apparently, whomever was in here last was not interested in them since they were still neatly stacked near the now defunct security gate.

Much of what was on the shelves had dropped on the floor, leaving me to wonder whether whomever had been in here last was looking for something, or simply trying to ransack the place.

Everyone spread out. I walked methodically down each aisle as quickly as I could, carefully looking at what was on the floor and what was left on the shelf, thinking of what could be of use. Realizing that we hadn't done exactly the greatest job before of predicting what we would need, I erred on the side of more.

The last place I looked was the pharmacy counter at the back. It should have been the first place I thought, but I wanted to keep an eye on the front of the store to see if we attracted any attention.

The counter was protected by a security grille. I stood in front of it, long enough that the others began to surround me, of who I was unaware until Joseph asked, "how are we going to open that?"

He kind of startled me. I grinned, "if they can get through the front door, we can get through this. Stay here," I said.

I went to the front door and peered out. I scanned the area, including from what I could see at the sides. It was largely silent outside, except for the wind, some birds, and the ticking of the car engine. I pressed the trunk button on the keychain and the trunk popped open. I walked outside, pulled the liner out of the trunk, and took the tire iron out from beside the spare tire.

I remembered it from when my family travelled to see some caves up north. We had blown a tire and my father made me watch as he changed it. My mother complained, however, it was on the passenger side of the vehicle and out of the way of traffic, so she begrudgingly agreed when my father bemoaned that I needed to learn such things. The absurdity was that

I hadn't even learned to drive yet, and he was teaching me how to change a tire.

"What's that?" Daniel asked as I entered the pharmacy.

"Hopefully our savior," I said sarcastically. I took the tire iron and wedged it between two of the horizontal bars and began to pull down. The bars bent. "How are we going to do this?" I exclaimed, already with a sense of defeat, my confidence quickly vanishing.

"Let me see it," Joseph said reaching out his hand. I handed it to him. He walked the length of the grille and stopped near the right-hand side where there was a keyed lock that fastened the security grille to the floor. He wedged the tire iron near the lock and pushed down on it. The lock snapped.

I crawled inside. "You guys stay there," I said looking back, "no point all of us getting trapped in," I muttered under my breath. I let out a sigh, for now I was faced with a wall of pills, all in white bottles and all with blue caps. I began reading the labels, "ari..., ari-prip..., yeah, I can't read these."

I looked behind me to see Joseph and Daniel both standing with their faces against the gate, their fingers intertwined with the metal, and looking as dumbstruck as I was.

"Maybe we should just take a bit of everything," Joseph said. It wasn't a bad idea, I thought staying silent. It's just, even if we did, we'd still have no idea what any of them were. I began filling my basket with one of each bottle, "it makes no sense though, there are like a thousand bottles here," I said before giving up.

"My mom gave me penicillin for an ear infection," Daniel blurted out.

"Penicillin," I said scanning the bottles. "At least they are in alphabetical order," I responded. "Nope, there's nothing with that name," I said when I reached the P's. It was getting dark. Even though the front of the pharmacy faced west, the sun was already dropping behind the houses and tree line.

"Screw it," I said as I began to just continue taking one of each bottle. "We can figure it out later." After about ten minutes, I had four baskets filled with at least a bottle of each drug. Perhaps I skipped over a few, losing my place here and there, but I figured, I had most of them.

I pushed the baskets through the opening and then squeezed back out myself. Joseph reached down and grabbed my hand to help me back to my feet. "We need to go," Joseph said. I nodded and we took the baskets back and forth to the trunk of the car. We piled in and drove back to the compound.

On the way back home, I let out a cough. "I'm alright," I said trying to pacify Joseph and Daniel who both seemed immediately concerned.

"You should get into the back with Daniel," I said to Joseph. "Why would I need to go back there?"

I then coughed again. I looked at him. He crawled over the seat and into the back.

Within thirty minutes, I was coughing more intensely, and my joints had begun to hurt. By the time we reached the compound, I was shivering from a fever. Daniel handed Joseph a surgical mask and gloves as we entered. "Did you get these?" Joseph asked and Daniel nodded. He rubbed Daniel's head in approval and even in my condition, I mustered up a smile.

Inside, about half of the kids were showing symptoms. Violet was handing out cups of hot water to people and Bella was going around and checking on everyone. Daniel handed Violet and Bella each a mask. They emptied the contents of the bags onto the floor and pulled out a few thermometer packages.

"Andrew's sick," Joseph said as he lay me down on the sofa. He came back with some water and a blanket, while Bella checked my temperature.

"It's 41 degrees!" Bella exclaimed. "Violet, we need some ice," she yelled.

Joseph removed the blanket again as I moaned in protest. I was shivering cold, colder than I had ever been, colder than I had remembered the first time I had the virus.

I had visions. I believed I had bitten off my fingers and could hear them crunching in my mouth and that blood was gushing from my hands. I fell in and out of reality. I could hear voices, but not the voices of those around me, but a droning sound, of uncertain words, repeating over and over.

Joseph began removing my clothes, right down to my underwear. Bella began placing the ice on my body, but I could not feel it. "My mother would do this when I had a fever," she said reassuringly. She then gave me a Tylenol and some water to sip.

I slowly turned my head to look at Joseph. He was crying. The boy who I knew to be calm and collected, a rock, was falling apart. He held my hand and I looked at his face, his brown eyes, his black hair, his lips that used to kiss me. I fell unconscious.

"Andrew, come," Joseph said opening the door to the compound.

"Where are we going, it's after dark?"

"You'll see," Joseph said taking my hand. It was past twilight, that time the mosquitos were no longer biting. The moon was full, which provided enough light for us to see through the forest that we were walking through. We walked eastward toward the boardwalk. He led me to the first observation deck, which had a good view of the lake, and we sat down on the bench.

"There are so many stars."

"Isn't it beautiful?" Joseph asked as he pulled my body close to his.

"In the city, we'd see maybe four or five on a good night."

The sky was black and dotted with countless stars and I wondered whether there were more stars than the space they occupied. Even the gasses were visible. The space around the circle of the moon turned from a light to navy blue.

While it had been a couple of months since we had come to Crawford Lake, this was the first time with everything going on that we were able to just sit and look at the sky. A part of me wished that we had brought everyone out here, another that we were alone.

"Do you know what any of these stars are?" I asked Joseph.

"Well, that's the big dipper," he said, pointing to what looked like a pot with a handle, "but that's all I know."

"I don't know what any of them are." We never learned anything about stars in school.

The light of the moon glimmered on the crystal-clear lake surface. Indeed, even the reflection of the shadows of trees in the moonlight cast upon the water. A dead silence fell over the lake, only interrupted by the occasional sound of waterfowl or some creature scurrying within the forest.

I could feel Joseph's heart beating through me. The air was mildly cool, and it would be enough to need a blanket if his arms were not wrapped around me.

The two of us sat silently. I used to spend a lot of time on the balcony at home, even at night. The city never slept. I would watch the shapes of other people on their balconies. I could hear their voices, but not so distinctly to hear what they were saying. So many lives, visible from my balcony, and here, it was just the two of us. Even when my family went camping, just a space away was another family, but here, besides ourselves and our family within the compound, the nearest person could be a mile or more away.

"I never saw you on the balcony," I said to Joseph. We had lived next door to each other for at least a year. He had moved in with his mother and our balconies were separated only by a glass divider. Unlike our balcony which had wooden tiles and our outdoor sofa, theirs remained empty.

"My mom was always working, and I was always at practice. We never really did anything outside. After my dad died, my mom had to work, and I just concentrated on basketball."

In a time gone by, I would have said that I was sorry or that it must be hard to lose a father, but for all of us now, it was reality, and I knew how it felt. This we all had in common. The only difference was the time that had passed.

We sat for hours without saying much else. At one point I drifted off, unknowing if he had done the same, but when I awoke, he held me tighter. The air smelled like the earthy forest mingled with the scent of him.

"I'm glad we're together," he said. "I mean, I'm glad that you came and got me." In honesty, if he hadn't made any noise, I wouldn't have remembered. It wasn't that I didn't know he was there, it's just that with everything that had happened, the situation, the isolation of being stuck within our homes, I was incapable of thinking of anything or anyone beyond myself. "I'm glad too," I answered. And I was, I was glad beyond measure.

Bella put some more ice on my body waking me up. I had been dreaming. She was so calm amongst all the chaos. I watched her as she walked around the room tending to everyone and after about twenty minutes, the shivering began to subside. Joseph came and sat closer beside me. He had stopped crying, but I could see he was distressed.

I just looked at him. I could not speak. I am unsure why. But he spoke to me, "you'll be okay," he said, over and over. He stroked my face with his hand, and I fell unconscious again.

I awoke the next morning and Joseph was still beside me, although he too had fallen asleep. I placed my hand on his head, which was resting on my bare stomach.

I was cold again, not from a fever, but rather because it really was cold. Some of the kids had not gotten sick and were still tending the others. My joints still hurt, and I felt weak. I tried to sit up.

"No, no, rest," Joseph said waking from my movement.

"I'm cold again," I said, although my mouth was dry, and I am sure it sounded completely different than it should have. Before I could protest, he went to grab a thermometer.

"Blanket," I said now uttering a single word instead of attempting a full sentence while reaching down to the floor.

Joseph took it and covered me and placed his hand on my forehead. "You're okay," he said as he tried to force a smile. I could see he was still concerned. "Do you want some water?" he asked putting it to my mouth without even waiting for a response.

I reached up toward his head and brought his ear down to my mouth.

"I love you," I whispered to him. He looked at me and smiled, but his eyes welled with tears.

"I love you too," he said almost with a laugh, and I could tell his tears were of happiness.

"Everyone else?" I asked looking around. He nodded his head.

"Don't worry about that right now," he said reassuringly.

I could see Brad sitting, leaning against the wall near the hallway to the office. He looked disengaged and I realized that this meant Anders probably didn't survive. I didn't say anything more. I succumbed to fatigue and once again fell back asleep.

I opened my eyes slightly and tried to speak. Bella was sitting on the floor surrounded by the medication we had taken from the pharmacy.

"Oh! You're awake! Are you hungry?" she asked looking in my direction.

"Where..." I began.

"Where is Joseph?" she said finishing my sentence. It wasn't what I was going to ask, but I nodded anyway. "He's just up top, they are digging..." she trailed off. I understood. They were burying Anders.

I tried to sit up when she lifted a cup of soup from the coffee table in front of me.

"You go easy," she said.

Every part of my body still ached. "Where is everyone?" I asked after taking a sip.

Only Luna was still in the living room, sitting on the couch across from me, covered in a blanket and drinking soup.

"They are all in the glass enclosure, well, except Violet, who is in the kitchen," she said. I could see her eyes roll slightly at the sound of metal pots and pans clunking around.

"You were asleep for quite a long time," Luna said before taking another sip of her soup.

"How long?" I asked, thinking that if Luna was making this statement, it must have been long.

"Two days," Bella said.

"Two *days*?" I asked repeating her in disbelief.

"Yup," she said.

"I'm still tired," I said.

"That's why you need to eat," she said putting the soup to my mouth again. I tried to hold the glass, but my hands were weak, and I couldn't keep it up to my mouth very long.

"I will go get Joseph," she said with a smile as she disappeared into the glass enclosure.

Joseph appeared, not from the glass enclosure, but through the front door. I imagined that Bella, who was still inside the glass enclosure, used the exit hatch to simply tell him that I was awake. He looked well. He walked at a quick pace and around to the couch. He threw the cushions off the back of the couch to make more room and lay facing me.

"How do you feel?" he asked as he pushed my hair from my forehead. He put his arm around my waist and his leg in between the two of my own, which made my lower back feel instantly better.

"I know how to stop the exodus," I said, having had a vision while I was feverish.

"How?" he asked.

"When we went to the library, well, anywhere, do you remember the virus posters?"

"Yeah," he said, waiting for me to continue.

"We should make some and post them through the forest informing people that this area is a burial site."

I saw the light in Joseph's face. I could tell that he loved the idea, even before he spoke. "This is an amazing idea!" he said sitting up. "That could actually work! We could also make a sign, for the compound and say that it is a burial building," he said. Neither Bella nor Luna seemed captivated by the idea.

"What's Bella doing?" I asked.

"I am making a list," she said. "While I've been here watching you and Luna, I've been trying to figure out what all these medications are for by looking in that book you got me from the library. I'm on the letter M, *Mupirocin*, is an anti-biotic for skin infections, and *Myambutol* is for tuberculosis." She struggled to pronounce the words and I had no idea whether she was saying them correctly or not. "The only problem is that I don't know what some of the medical words mean. I didn't know what *tuberculosis* was."

"It's something to do with the lungs," Joseph replied.

"Yeah, well, I know that now," Bella said agitatedly having figured that out on her own. She was always happy but had a sarcastic tone to everything she said.

"I think it's great," Joseph said, "having a list that you can look down."

"Rather than have to figure out everything from a giant medical book?" she said laughing.

"You should try to make a list by body part too," I said. She seemed receptive to this, but I could see that she was a bit disappointed by my suggestion, being half-way through the medication already.

The rest of the day, I could hear Mia, Daniel, and Brad in the office talking about how to change the poster they were creating and make it more convincing. Their words were muddled by the echo in the hallway as they talked over each other. Violet would sometimes pitch in when she brought them food or snacks to eat, which I suspect she was doing more than usual so she could be involved.

Joseph would occasionally check on them, but his primary focus was me. He spent the afternoon sitting beside me, reading me a mystery novel he had found in the library. I figured that's why he spent so much time in the fiction section. Either way, I never asked as I enjoyed the company and the serenity of his voice.

The next time he left my side, he came back with a copy of the flyer and showed me what they had so far.

"It looks amazing! How did they get the government logo?" I exclaimed.

"Can I see?" Luna asked and Joseph handed it to her. "That is *amazing*," Luna responded.

"Brad found a flyer on the doors of the visitor center, and they scanned it." I thought, this could work. "We will find some wood and make a sign to attach to the compound door tomorrow, I figured the flyer is enough for them to handle today," Joseph said trying to inject some humor.

As the day went on, I drifted in and out of sleep. Joseph was beside me, either sleeping or talking to the other kids.

The next morning, I was feeling better and when I awoke, Joseph grabbed me some food and drink from the kitchen. "Are you hungry?" he asked kneeling beside the couch and giving me the plate of food. "Starved," I said.

After eating, he helped me into the shower. Even though it wasn't the first time he had seen me naked, I still felt awkward. Afterwards he helped stable me and then dried me off.

I brushed my teeth, which felt absolutely disgusting, and then went back to the living room and spent the day sitting on the couch watching the younger kids.

This gave Mia a much-needed break. She worked so hard I thought, and oftentimes, I was so preoccupied with things that I took it for granted. Joseph disappeared with Brad up top to put up the flyers they had printed. Time would tell whether my idea would work.

CHAPTER

Seventeen

I BARELY NOTICED AS Brad entered the compound. I was still recovering on the couch and Joseph, who was sitting beside me, had begun reading another chapter from the mystery novel. The book was about a young girl who went missing in the highlands of Scotland and a detective had been assigned to the case to find her. And with Joseph reading, in his calming voice, I never wanted him to stop.

"I found something," Brad said, coming around to the couch and kneeling on the floor in front of us. I felt annoyed, simply because the book was just getting good, and I was still too tired and weak to deal with the drama I knew was coming. But before either Joseph or I could ask, Brad uttered something even more captivating than the book, "a door."

Joseph put the book down and leaned forward intrigued, resting his arms on his legs, and clasping his hands together.

"What do you mean?" I asked, my throat still dry and my voice breaking.

"About a kilometer, north-west of here, among some bushes, there is a metal door."

"Did you open it?" Joseph asked.

"The code didn't work."

"It has a code?" I asked. He nodded.

"Another compound?" I asked trying to lift myself up from the couch. I lost my balance and fell slightly back.

"You should rest," Joseph said.

"We need to find the code," I replied standing up once again. I was a bit shaky, but my sturdiness improved with each step.

I walked to my father's office and Joseph followed me. We looked at the papers, within the drawers. There were numbers written on some, but none resembled a combination.

"I can't find anything," Brad said defeatedly walking into the office after looking around the others, "and I take it from the looks on your faces, neither did either of you."

"Not yet," Joseph said, unwilling to admit defeat.

I sat in my father's chair, gently rocking it back and forth. I spun around and it was then that I saw it. Behind my father's desk on the sideboard, there was a photo of he and I at a Toronto Blue Jay's game from last year. Although I never liked sports, it was one of those times where my father felt the need to make up for all the times that he was not at home.

He had come home one day after being away for several and produced a pair of Blue Jay's tickets. In his hand, he had a couple of jerseys, one for him and one for me. It didn't fit too well; I swam in it.

I presumed that he hoped my love for baseball would catch on and I would grow into it. My jersey was for Ryan Borucki, number 56 and his was for Danny Jansen, number 9. I stared at the picture long enough that both Joseph and Brad caught on. "I think I know the number," I said, "it's 5609."

We put on our shoes and even though it was warm out, Joseph insisted that I wear a jacket. I didn't have the energy to object. We walked through the forest in the direction of the door, letting Brad lead the way. It was rough going and rather exhausting.

The land gave way to a small ravine. It was lined with bushes and large boulders of limestone on either side. The ravine directed us downward toward a metal door embedded within the face of the earth. It wasn't well hidden, but not entirely visible either. Like the compound, the door had an electronic keypad that gave off the same green glow.

I tried entering the combination. It took a second before the keypad beeped green and the door slid open. The light went on automatically and we found ourselves staring down a long hallway.

"What the hell is this?" Brad asked somberly.

"It looks like it goes on forever," Joseph said. Although we couldn't tell, because the lights in the distance were off and the light faded to darkness.

Lining the hallway were small empty rooms. Each room had a sliding glass door with the familiar white hand symbol, a number in the same white coating, and the same shower symbol that was in the terrarium.

"What's that for?" Brad asked. I looked at Joseph and smirked.

"It's for showering," I replied.

"How'd you know that?" he questioned.

"A hunch," I laughed.

We entered one of the rooms, which was made entirely of concrete and coated in a glass-like material. There were no edges, and the walls, ceiling, and floor seamlessly rounded into each other. The ceiling omitted a soft white glow that lit up the room. Embedded within the middle of the floor was a drain and above it, on the ceiling, was a shower head.

At the back of the room was another glass door that led into another hallway.

"What is this place?" Brad asked inquisitively.

"Whatever it is, it looks unfinished," Joseph said.

"It looks like a hospital," I said, and I could tell my response made them both pause and think, however, there were no beds and no medical devices.

"Maybe, it's quarters for sleeping," Brad said.

"But why the shower heads?" Joseph asked.

"Okay, so not for sleeping," Brad responded.

We walked down the main hallway until we reached a large circular room, a hub of sorts that connected the main and two side hallways. The room itself was empty and the walls and floors bare. It was clearly unfinished. Bags of concrete lay on the floor along with a mixer and some tools. Several large rectangular openings embedded within the wall were stacked on top of each other.

We continued walking to the end of the hallway. The last room had the number '100' on it and in front of us, stood a metal door, that led outside. When we opened the door, it was surrounded by dense shrubbery and bushes. We would have had to climb our way out.

"I wonder where this door is?" I asked. But I could tell that none of us had the answer and none of us were feeling adventurous enough to get injured by the thorny thickets that stood before us.

We walked back to the main entrance.

"Maybe we can sleep here instead," Joseph said, "these rooms could be bedrooms." I remained silent as I mulled his idea over.

"But there are no washrooms here," Brad replied. "We wouldn't want to be walking back and forth to the compound every time we needed to use the washroom."

"Good point," Joseph said.

"Maybe you can keep your rabbits and chickens here for the time being," I said.

"I can do that," Brad responded.

I was feeling more energetic, possibly because of what Brad had discovered. We tried to find the exit, following the general direction of the second compound beneath us, but the vegetation was so dense that it seemed impossible.

"We can throw something out the door and look for it tomorrow," Joseph said. That was a great idea, I thought.

"How did they build this?" Brad asked. He was right, the entire area was undisturbed, and yet beneath all the trees, rocks, and earth lay these compounds. They would have required backhoe's, cement trucks, dump trucks, and yet, there was no evidence of any of these.

"It's a good question," Joseph said. But like all the other questions, there were few answers, I thought.

When we arrived back at the main compound, we told the others of our discovery over dinner. Violet had made some soup and some rationed crackers, which I crushed and poured over top. There were never enough crackers, I thought.

After dinner, I left the lot and went and sat in my father's office and once again stared at the picture on the sideboard. I missed my dad. We never spent enough time together and that made it all the harder.

Joseph came. "Get up for a second," he said.

"Why?" I asked, but he simply smiled and waved his hand upward. I stood up, he sat, and then pulled me down to sit in his lap. He wrapped his arms around me. The warmth of his body felt good, and it was a welcome reprieve from all the walking that we did.

I swiped the strip on my father's desk turning on the screens and pressed the icon for the map.

"The dots," I said pointing, "on the map, do you think they are compounds? I mean, they must be."

"Maybe. But there are so many," Joseph replied. The nearest dot was in North Bay and although I had heard of this place, I had never been anywhere that far north, and it seemed too far for us to visit. "It's too far," he said verbalizing what I was already thinking.

"Maybe someday we should try though," I said.

"It would be really risky, and it would take days," he said. "It's also just a pin in a city. We'd have no idea where in that city the compound was."

I nodded. He was right, there was no way for us to know. The dot for Crawford Lake could have been anywhere in kilometers of land, without my father's map, we wouldn't have found it. There had to be a reason these compounds existed though, and why there were so many of them. I tried figuring out if it were possible to show more information on a particular dot, but there was nothing.

The next morning, I contemplated getting up, but I was comfortable in my secluded spot under the desk. I could tell that I slept in from the noise of the kids echoing about the halls.

About ten minutes or so later, Joseph entered the room and knelt in the opening of the desk while balancing on the toes of his feet. He had one hand on the top of the desk and the other perched over his legs allowing his hand to dangle in between.

"Good morning."

"Hi," I said quietly still in the boundary between being asleep and awake.

"I found where the other door leads."

I sat up slightly, not wanting to hit my head, "Where?"

"Not far from the back of this compound."

"Really?"

"Yeah."

"Let me get up and you can show me," I said to him enthusiastically.

As I began to arise, he pulled down a plate that he had put on top of the desk and was holding with his other hand. "Not before you eat," he said handing it to me as he grinned.

"How do you feel?" he asked me as I began to eat.

"Much better," I said. It wasn't entirely truthful, but I didn't want to be a shut in today. I needed the fresh air.

"That's good, I'm glad," he said with a smile brushing away my hair from my temple.

I wasn't used to getting a lot of attention like this. In school, no one even batted an eye at me. "Did you notice me in school?" I asked him inquisitively.

He looked away and let out a grin. Tears welled slightly in his eyes. He was emotional. He nodded. I put down my plate of food and pulled him into my chest. He continued to nod his head before saying, "yes."

"How come you never spoke to me?" I asked.

"How come you never spoke to *me*?" He laughed gently pushing me away.

"Then it was fate," I said.

"Don't think this will get you out of eating your food," he joked, reaching down and stuffing some more in my mouth.

Joseph led me to the back door of the northern compound. It was covered with brush and mostly inaccessible compared to the front entrance.

"The back door of the main compound is over there," Joseph said pointing. I squinted, unable to see it. "It's covered by all that dirt," he said. All I could see was a slight hint of grey amongst the dark earth and green foliage.

"It'll be a nightmare to clear," I said. He nodded.

"I wonder if we should even clear it though," Joseph said, "maybe it is meant to be hidden?" He stepped down into the brush slightly and looked around the area. I figured he was gauging what people might be able to see if we were to clear it.

"Maybe we can join them together?" I asked. The distance between the two doors was about twenty meters. Not impossible I thought.

"It would be an undertaking," he said, "what would we use to connect them?"

"Whatever would be easiest for us to find and carry," I responded.

"So, we wouldn't use concrete then?" he asked.

I shook my head unsure. "I mean we could, but don't you think that would be a lot of work? I was thinking metal culverts or plastic tube slides or even wooden boards."

He nodded.

I felt less enthusiastic at this moment. It was one thing to think about doing something than to actually do it. I definitely didn't have the energy or resolve to do it today.

"Maybe we can go back inside," I said.

"Too much?" he asked.

"Yeah," I nodded. "Maybe we can go into the terrarium?"

"Sure," he said.

We walked back to the compound and went to the terrarium elevator. We waited until no one was watching, entered, and descended.

"At some point we should tell them that we were able to get in here," Joseph said.

"Yeah," I responded, "just not yet."

The showering process was no more enjoyable the second time around. When we entered, I took my time, not because I was tired and really wanted to sleep, but because I wanted to be thorough.

"The path," I said looking at Joseph.

"What about it?"

"It shows us where it wants us to go, but maybe we need to get off the path and go into the growth, what do you think?"

"We don't really know what's in there," he said apprehensively.

"We don't, but why would they plant it all if whomever entered had to stick to a path?" He paused. I didn't want to push him. "We have so many questions and we need to find answers."

At this Joseph took my hand with resolve and we entered the brush. It wasn't easy going. Some plants simply glided across our bodies, while others stung and jabbed. He picked up a stick and used it to push the branches out of our way as we walked.

"What are we looking for?" Joseph asked me.

"I dunno. Let's go up there," I said to him pointing east, "all the way to the edge."

We walked east, pushing our way through the growth as it started to rain. Since we weren't following a trail, it was more difficult of a walk. There was more wildlife, including insects, which I whisked off my body as I felt them land on my skin. I hated insects. And then we hit it.

The wall was almost invisible, just like the shell of the elevator. If it weren't for Joseph's stick, we would have probably walked right into it. It was mirror like, but it didn't show our reflection. He tapped it with the stick he was holding, and bright rainbow-colored lines emanated from the point, quickly diffusing. "It reminds me of when I hit our television at home," I said, louder because of the rain. "I was thinking the same thing," he said. Joseph tapped a few different places, as high up as he could reach, and it was the same.

"This entire place, this entire dome, is like a giant TV," he said. But it wasn't a television. That, I was pretty sure of.

"So now what?" Joseph asked.

I stood still looking up as far as I could see. The edges of the dome disappeared in the mist. It was impossible to see the curvature that we both knew was there.

"Let's walk around the edge," I said.

"Okay," he responded as he led, tapping the sides of the dome with the stick as we went.

The rain was beginning to taper off again when we reached a swampy area lined with reeds. The hard ground had begun to turn to mud. The mud oozed around my toes and felt cooler than the surrounding air. Small bubbles glided up from the mud through the water.

"Have you ever been to a place like this?" I asked Joseph, "I mean to a jungle."

He shook his head, "we never really went anywhere, my mother and me. She was always working, and I was always focusing on sports. We never had the money or time to go anywhere. How about you?" he asked.

"Never," I responded.

"How come you never came on school trips?" he asked. He had noticed.

"Overprotective father," I responded.

"I was always hoping that you would come," he said before continuing to walk.

The reeds around the swamp made it difficult to gauge the size of it.

"Let's go around," Joseph said walking away from the dome wall around the swamp. Invisible to our eye, frogs croaked always from a distance, silencing themselves as we approached.

Near the north-western side of the swamp, there was a large outlet that fed into a stream. The water was clear and transitioned across the muddy bottom of the swamp to the rocky bottom of the stream. The stream was rather wide and deep, but we helped each other across safely.

We continued to walk, but it wasn't long until we once again hit the dome wall. It was there that we found a door. It was hidden, much like the elevator, but still visible around the edges.

Joseph and I looked at each other, "should we go in?" he asked.

I nodded.

The door led to an elevator. The elevator descended a couple of stories. Unlike the others, it was enclosed in metal and not glass, preventing us from seeing outside. Perhaps there was nothing to see. The door opened and we found ourselves in a rectangular room full of large metal pipes and pumps.

"This must be what controls everything," Joseph said.

The room was immaculately clean. There were six pumps, numbered on the wall behind them. Some pumps were operating, and others were silent. The pipes had yellow arrows on them, which we assumed was the direction of whatever was flowing inside of them. Some were labeled 'WHITE WATER, GREY WATER, and BLACK WATER.' Neither of us knew what those meant.

The wall closest to the elevator was made of a white, glass-like material. On it were displayed two screens. One showed the pumps found within the room, colored in either red, yellow, or green. We managed to quickly figure out that the green pumps were operating, and the red pumps were not. We had no idea what the yellow pumps represented since they appeared to be operating.

The other screen showed a map of the terrarium and for the first time we grasped just how massive it all was. We inspected the map thoroughly as Joseph pointed to the various landmarks that we had already seen. Each had names, but the names were not like those that we'd heard before.

The swamp was named, "Edom." The stream that flowed from it, was named "Pishon." The large body of water surrounding the platform and stairs was named, "Siloam."

"What's with all of these names?" Joseph asked.

"I dunno," I responded. They were difficult to pronounce and remember.

"What's this button do?" Joseph asked pressing an icon on the screen. The screen changed to a list of animal species. Mammals, Birds, Reptiles, Amphibians, Fish, and Invertebrates.

We both mumbled the names under our breaths. Joseph tapped 'Mammals' and a list of mammals appeared. "Agouti, Squirrel, Vampire Bat, Coati, ..." he mumbled off.

"These are all the animals in here?" I asked.

"They are probably afraid of us and keep away," Joseph responded.

We left the mechanical room. The light in the terrarium was fading. We walked the same direction in which we came, following the border of the swamp and dome back to the elevator.

We showered the black mud off our bodies, got dressed, and ascended to the main floor.

"Are we still keeping it a secret?" Joseph asked.

I nodded.

"Where have you two been?" Mia asked as we entered the living room area.

"Out and about," I responded nonchalantly.

"Is everything okay?" Joseph asked.

"Funny, I was out all day and never saw either of you," Brad said.

"What?" I asked defensively.

"We found strawberries!" Luna said changing the subject.

"Strawberries?" I asked.

"Yeah, Brad took me out and we found some along the trail."

"We are having them for dessert," Violet said getting up and walking toward the kitchen.

"Did you notice anything?" Brad asked me. I looked around expecting something.

"No," I responded.

"I moved the surplus supplies to the North Compound today."

"Oh, wow," Joseph said, "that's good."

"Yeah, Mia and I felt it would give us some more space."

"Did you all eat?" I asked Violet, as she returned with two plates.

"We already ate," Violet said.

Dinner was cold.

CHAPTER

Eighteen

I WAS SITTING AT the desk in my father's office, swiveling on the chair. My elbows lay on the leather arm rests and my hands were clasped together with my index fingers on my lips. I was deep in thought when Joseph walked in.

"What are you up to? I got caught trying to break up an argument between Madison and Daniel and when I turned around you were gone."

"I'm realizing I didn't know much about my father," I sighed after a moment's thought. When I said 'much', I should have said, 'anything'. "I mean, he would go away for days at a time for work, but I never knew where. And we came here, to Crawford Lake so many times, and all this time, he knew that right underneath us, this place existed."

Joseph just remained silent and sat on the edge of the desk. He watched with an empathetic expression.

"I don't understand any of this stuff," I said, dramatically pushing aside some of the folders that I had placed on the desk. He knelt and put his hand on my arm. "All of these formulas and notes might as well be in French!"

"Tu ne parles pas français?" Joseph said with a grin.

"Ha-ha, I flunked French."

"You failed French?"

"Failed a lot of things actually."

"I always thought you were good at school, you seemed to know the answers when the teacher called on you."

"I'm more interested in music," I said. I missed it. I had just been too caught up in everything to think about it until now.

"Let me have a look," he said, grabbing a stack of folders and sitting down on the floor next to my chair.

He opened the first one. He was so focused, I wondered if he understood any of it. "Do you understand this stuff?"

"Nope, but I'm not against trying," he said. I sighed, grabbed the next folder, and began looking over it again.

After about ten minutes, I had given up again, and put the folders back haphazardly on the desk. I laid back in my chair and resumed twisting it from side to side. Joseph placed the folder down on his lap and looked at me.

"Your father was a virologist, Andrew."

"What's that?" I asked, stopping my twirling by placing a foot on the floor.

"He worked with viruses."

"Where'd you learn that word?"

"It's here, it's written in this pamphlet," he said handing it to me. The pamphlet had some pictures of people, one of who was my father and sure enough, under his picture, it said 'Virologist'.

"Viruses?" I said flabbergasted. "Do you think that this is what this place is?" I asked.

After a few minutes of flipping through some more documents, he continued, "actually, I think your father was working on *this* virus." I laughed, but he didn't.

"You're serious?" I asked sitting up in the chair.

"Yup, I think so," he said reading from a letter:

"All efforts to reverse the spread of the pandemic have failed. It has spread to all continents on the planet. Fatalities have reached into the billions. The survival rate amongst children under the age of twelve is 80% and that

of all other age groups is 0.05%. Vaccines and antivirals are ineffectual in combating the virus and our ability to create a timely vaccine has been hindered by its rapid spread. It is recommended that all personnel abandon efforts and spend whatever time they have left with their families."

"But how is that possible?" I responded, mildly angry.

"I don't know, but it's what it says," he responded calmly.

"I don't understand what any of this is though," I said frustratingly.

"It's okay, just skip over the parts that don't make sense, and try to understand what does," he said in his calm voice and at this, I felt reinvigorated.

Another hour passed without us saying anything to each other. I had changed positions in the chair several times trying to get comfortable, but Joseph remained composed and focused.

"I think I understand what I am looking at," I said to Joseph, still uncertain of myself.

"What's that?"

"These are the results of tests. Look at this one, it says 'non-reactive', actually, they all do, all these papers, on all of these dates." He smiled at me. "What?"

"You're becoming impassioned," he said.

I couldn't help but laugh a little. "Non-reactive means, at least I think it means, that the antidote they were looking for had failed."

Joseph nodded. "I think so too," he said looking at the papers. "But what are all of these names?" he asked.

I looked at the next piece of paper and answered flatly, "they are people."

"But there are so many."

"I can't look at this anymore today!" I said frustratingly, standing up and leaving the papers on the chair before walking out of the room.

"Hey, hey wait," he said standing up and coming after me. As I turned, he just held me in his arms.

"What does all this mean? What does it all mean?" I cried.

"Nothing. It doesn't mean anything. We already know that there were many compounds just like this one, which means your father wasn't working alone. They were probably all trying to fix it, to find a cure, but..." I knew what he meant. No one found a cure because everyone died. And not just here, but everywhere. There were no planes, no helicopters, no cars, and anyone we did see was young.

"Let's go sit by the lake," he said.

"We should get Luna."

"Sure," he said rubbing my hair with a laugh to lighten the mood and we did.

We sat on the boardwalk of Crawford Lake, a little way in. We were somewhat hidden by the foliage and so anyone that might be in the area wouldn't be able to see us.

"I hate that it has to be this way, that we have to worry about other people," I said.

"I do too," Joseph said. It used to be when I walked in the forest and saw people, I would say 'hi' and they would respond in kind. Now, it seemed we had to worry about their intent – were they friendly, or not. It used to be safe and now it was all uncertain.

The sky was clear and the only clouds that I could see were in the distance. It was one of those cool days and Joseph stayed close to me, but I wasn't sure if that were the reason or whether he simply just wanted to stay close to me. Either way, I was good with it.

Behind us, Luna was walking around trying to identify more plants. "There's not much new here," she grumbled.

"Let's take a walk around the boardwalk then," Joseph said, and we began walking south. He clasped my hand in his and held it tight. He looked at me and intentionally blinked with both eyes while smiling.

We kept our wits about us, trying to keep quiet and stay alert. We walked slow as Luna was keenly looking from side to side to see if there were any plants she hadn't seen before. I could sense her frustration grow if we didn't give her enough time to look.

At the southmost end of the boardwalk, there was a swampy area. We sat on the observation deck allowing Luna to look at the various wetland plants that existed there.

"This is poisonous nightshade," she said pointing to the orange, yellow, and green berries that dangled from the plant.

"Huh," I said in disbelief, "how do you know that?"

"They were in my book on Ontario Plants," she responded casually.

I was fascinated by her increasing knowledge but was slightly skeptical. How would any of us know without confirming it ourselves? The sight of them made me crave peppers though, since they were in the same assorted colors. I loved eating them raw and missed them.

Joseph sat with his legs up and his back rested against the railing and pulled me into him, so that I was laying down with my back against his chest.

"I want to find wild rice," Luna exclaimed.

"Wild rice?" Joseph asked.

"Yes, one of my books says it grows in wetlands in Ontario."

"Really?" Joseph sounded surprised.

"We have rice," I said cynically.

Joseph sensed how this might demotivate her and nodded at me, "but it would be good for the future, I mean when we run out."

"Yeah, totally," I chimed in. Although I believed rice would have been one of the last things we'd run out of.

Luna was too busy looking at the shoreline to listen to either of us banter. "Well, there's nothing else here, can we keep walking?" she asked impatiently. Both Joseph and I chuckled, and I followed his lead as we continued to walk around the boardwalk.

We began to circle back north along the eastern side of the lake. The forest was dark and most of the area was clear and devoid of any plant-life except trees. Luna walked faster, there was simply nothing new that interested her.

"We need to find a way to get everyone out of the compound, even if in groups," I said to Joseph. "Luna is right, when the winter comes, everyone will go stir crazy if they aren't already."

"We will need to think of something," Joseph said.

There wasn't much else of interest as we walked north along the boardwalk.

"Just wait a few minutes," I said to Luna as we stopped at an observation deck to take note of the area and see if anyone else was around.

"Do you hear something?" Joseph asked. My ears played tricks on me, and I could hear what I thought were the voices of others in the wind. I shook my head.

"I can't get over how invisible everything is," I said to Joseph looking across the lake. The main compound was buried under the white limestone cliffs that emerged from the water on the other side of the lake, capped with trees. Everything looked as right as rain.

"Me too," he said.

"Can we keep walking now?" Luna asked interrupting us. The shoreline beneath the observation deck didn't have anything new for her to look at and she was quickly becoming impatient.

Joseph smiled, and I could sense him withholding a laugh, "sure," he responded.

We continued to walk north until we reached another swampy area near the end of the boardwalk. We stayed there for an hour or so. There was enough plant life to keep Luna interested at least.

The area had been blocked off by official virus signs asking people to keep their distance from each other, but we ignored them and climbed over the railing. "We can go out again tomorrow," I said when she appeared finished, and we walked south back to the compound, the way we came.

When we returned, I settled back at my father's desk. I never felt we had much of a relationship when he was alive, and now, I felt as though, I had known him even less. The papers, at least those written in his handwriting, gave me a sense of connection, even though I didn't understand much of the scientific mumbo jumbo that was contained within them.

"Where are the bodies?" I asked Joseph when he joined me in the room.

"What do you mean?" Joseph asked.

"Well, all these people are non-reactive, and there are so many. No one survived, so, where are they all?"

"Maybe they were just blood samples, sent in from elsewhere," he replied after a minute.

That's true I thought, "could be."

"Maybe they were planning on having people in that building they built."

"But there's no road there, no way to get people or even bodies into that place, it's so isolated, maybe it wasn't a hospital," I replied. Neither of us clearly had any idea. "I guess it's not important," I said defeatedly. Because at this point both of us were just speculating on something we knew nothing about.

I started looking at the contents of every folder I could find, even those on Joseph's lap.

"What are you looking for?" he asked.

"Anything. Wait what's this?" I asked, opening a folder that contained some drawings. Joseph sat up a little, perched on his feet to get enough height to look at what was in the folder on my lap.

"It's a drawing." I rolled my eyes slightly at his stating the obvious.

"Of the compounds, but there's not two, there's *three*." I left the chair and knelt beside him, placing the drawings on the floor. "Here we are, and

this is the north compound. But on the drawing, it is called Wormwood."
I paused and remained still, before falling back slightly into a more relaxed
position on the floor.

"What is it?" Joseph asked me, putting his hand on my shoulder, like he
often did.

"It's just, I've heard that name before, 'Wormwood'."

"When?" he asked.

"My mom, she was religious, unlike my dad, and would often read her
Bible and she mentioned 'Wormwood' before." I paused a moment again
trying to remember the exact words, mumbling slightly so that Joseph
knew I hadn't yet finished speaking. "I can't remember the verse, and I
doubt there is a Bible in this place," I said throwing up my hands, "but
it referred to many people dying from the water, because it was bitter –
Wormwood means bitter."

"Why couldn't it just say something simple?" he asked. I smirked, which
made him laugh a little.

"And the main compound is called 'Eden'," I said. "Okay, my father
definitely wasn't religious."

"Maybe your mother knew?" Joseph asked. Although I doubted my
mother knew anything of this, it's possible she just didn't want to say
anything to me. I mean, I knew so little of my own father I thought.

"Maybe," I answered uncertain of myself.

"And then there's this," Joseph said pointing to the third building on
the map.

"Where is that?" I asked him.

"Well, here's the lake," he said, and it even said 'Crawford Lake' on the
drawing. "And here's the boardwalk around the lake. And then, there's a
path that goes eastward." I watched his finger trace the dotted line on the
map east toward the third building.

"Nassagaweya Canyon," I said trying to pronounce the word, with great
difficulty.

"Nassa-ga-wey-a," Joseph said correcting me. I smiled.

"I've been there. There are these giant birds, called Turkey Vultures, that fly above the canyon. There are also caverns, and lots of trees and plants."

"Luna's dream," Joseph said.

"Definitely," I said as we both laughed. "But I've never seen a building there," I said.

"Does that surprise you?" Joseph asked.

"Not anymore," I responded realizing the irony in what I was saying.

I pulled another diagram from the folder. It was of Wormwood. I began to shake. "What's wrong?" Joseph asked me as he took the diagram from my hands. I sat back against the wall without saying anything. "Crematorium," he said aloud when he read it.

"It's where they burn dead people. My father was a monster."

We didn't tell anyone where we were going. It was just Joseph and me. The thought of not having left at least a note toyed with my mind, but we had already left. We were always doing this, going places without letting anyone know.

I had mulled bringing Luna, but I knew that we would be too preoccupied to keep an eye on her and the cliffs were dangerous, with deep crevasses that any one of us could get injured in.

We headed out across the woods toward the northern shore of Crawford Lake. Everything was still, and a slight mist arose from the surface of the water, reducing our visibility.

After reaching the shore, we continued eastward on the trail. I had been on it before. The vegetation was different along the trail. Small streams crossed the path and led into swampy areas. I stepped over them as best I could to avoid getting muddy. There were lots of ferns and rocks that lay at the base of the tall trees and bushes.

"Luna would be happy here," Joseph said.

"It's lucky we didn't bring her, as we would never make it anywhere near the canyon," I laughed.

"Shh-shh-shh," he said kneeling. Just steps in front of us was an orange newt.

"Do you think it is poisonous?"

"I dunno."

"It's orange," I said, "doesn't that mean it is poisonous?"

"Maybe," he said reaching out.

"No!" I shouted, but before I could stop him, he had picked it up and was holding it in his hand. I grasped my head in my hands and pulled on my hair in frustration.

"He's okay, aren't you little guy?"

Joseph placed the newt back on the ground and it scurried into the bushes. We walked along the path, and I noticed a peculiar plant with a red berry encased within a pink thorny shell.

"Oh, this is interesting," I said to Joseph as I knelt to look at it. "I wonder what it is?" I asked.

"I'm sure Luna would know," he said, "or could find out."

I picked part of the plant along with the fruit. "I'm going to take one back with us," I said placing the berry within my pocket. "I just hope I don't forget it's in there."

We continued to walk along the trail until we reached the canyon. I led him by the hand, our fingertips entwined, down the path to the edge of the cliff. The edge was lined with a fence made of wood and stone pillars.

I looked out over the canyon at the sky. "There," I said pointing up, "Turkey Vultures." I looked at him and he was smiling, but he wasn't looking at them, he was looking at me. "Not at me, look," I said encouragingly. "Look at how huge they are, look at the trees and then see how big their wings are by comparison," I said to him.

"Wow," he replied nodding his head. I then kissed him on the hand, and he smiled and put his arm around me.

I looked down at the map and then at the area around us.

"I've been here, several times, right where we are standing," I said.

"It looks like the compound is near the cliff," Joseph said concentrating on the diagram. "It doesn't show this rest area though."

I looked at the diagram again, "no, it doesn't."

Of course, probably hundreds of tourists visited this area every day in the summer months and any compound within this area would have to be well hidden not to be noticed. I looked at the face of the cliff.

"I know the cliff curves around to the left of us," I said to Joseph, "and that is shown on the diagram. I think we need to walk south some more along the trail."

We walked south along the trail somewhat. The trail was shown on the map to some extent, as a dotted line and we noticed that the forest to the left of us was furthering us from the cliff edge and was thickening.

"I bet it is in there," I said to Joseph.

"Let's go in," he replied.

We walked within the forest, pushing our way through the bushes. "We have to watch for crevasses," I said holding him. I was more fearful of him falling into one that I was of myself.

We eventually came across a long crevasse that ran north-south, parallel to the canyon.

"Let's go north a bit," I said, and we walked north to where the crevasse began, and it was there that we saw it. On the eastside of the crevasse, there was a door. "Another keypad," I said, "here goes nothing." I entered '1102' and after a second the indicator light turned green, and the door opened.

"I wonder why Wormwood had a different entry code?" Joseph asked. It was a good question, to which I didn't have an answer.

Just inside the door, there was an elevator, with no added space but. Both Joseph and I looked at each other.

"What should we do?" he asked. I paused a moment. No one even knew where we were, but curiosity got the better of me.

"Let's go in," I replied.

I pressed the first button, there was only one. A few seconds later, the door opened, and we entered the elevator. There were several buttons. I looked at the display, 'G' was currently displayed.

"We are at Ground," I said.

"Let's go to each floor," Joseph said, and I pressed 'L1', which I assumed stood for 'Level One'.

The inside of the elevator had glass walls and a metal bar ran waist height around its perimeter. The glass walls were simply staring at the rock face of the cliffs that surrounded the elevator and I feared what would happen if any of the rock face were to fall and hit the glass.

A few seconds later, the door opened into a laboratory, interrupting my thoughts. Joseph and I were paralyzed, long enough that the door began to close before Joseph put his foot out to stop it.

The floor was covered with white tiles, but there was no grout between them. White cabinets with drawers and a light gray counter surrounded the entire perimeter of the lab. In the middle of the lab there was a large white workbench covered with a metallic glasslike surface. The entire room was bright and well-lit and full of computers, vials, microscopes, and other equipment. We pressed the white hand symbol next to the elevator and pressed 'L2'.

The elevator descended further than before, perhaps several stories down, and stopped within the middle of a room, allowing us to see through the sides and back before the door even opened. "We must be under the cliff, under the ground," I said.

The elevator door opened, and we immediately began heaving from the smell. We fumbled to press the close button. The room was lined with cages containing different animals, primates, rats, and birds. No one had survived to tend them, and all the animals were long dead.

"Let's get out of here," Joseph said as he knelt on all fours. I pressed 'G', knelt, and stroked his back with my hand.

When we reached ground, we were both quick to bolt out of the elevator, through the metal door and into the light. We gasped in the clean forest air, but I was certain the smell would linger with us for a while.

"What the hell?" Joseph yelled, angrily. I knew he wasn't angry at me. "Ugh," he moaned still retching from the smell. I stood still as he walked around animated. I had never seen him like this. "I never want to go back there," he yelled pointing. He looked like he was going to vomit as he hunched over and rested his hands on his knees.

I waited for him to calm down. "You okay?" I asked. He nodded. "Let's not tell anyone about this," I said. He nodded and we began walking back to Eden.

"Do you think they were testing the virus?" I blurted out. It took a few minutes for him to respond, and I felt that perhaps I shouldn't have said anything.

"Possibly to find a cure," Joseph responded, "either way, what was going on there was..." he stopped talking.

"You're not angry at me, are you?" I asked. Although after I said it, I wasn't sure why I said it.

"Of course not Andrew!" he snapped, "your father's sins are not your own!"

A few seconds later, he put his arm around my shoulder. I could feel he needed to show me he wasn't angry with me. I knew that it wasn't my fault, but I felt responsible for what my father was involved with. I was ashamed of his actions.

Still a part of me wanted to know more about what was in that lab. We had exhausted understanding most of what was in his office and that lab may have contained clues. But I felt now was not the time to bring it up.

We made it back to the beach on the north-side of the lake. Swimming was forbidden, although I'd seen people take their dogs off leash, allowing them to wade into the water. I always hated that. Humans seem to mess up everything, which was evident from the lab. Sure, Joseph had been in the lake, but that was different, life was now different. Before, I thought Crawford Lake was this pristine and unspoiled place, until I realized my father was working in a clandestine laboratory hidden underneath it, on the very virus that killed our loved ones and most humans on the planet.

Joseph was right, there would be no point ever visiting any of the other sites. They would be so well hidden that we would never be able to find them without detailed directions.

My legs struggled to balance as we walked through the sand.

"You alright?" he asked, as I almost, fell grabbing one of my hands.

I laughed, "yup."

We walked through the start of the western path toward the boardwalk past the Crawford house.

As soon as my foot landed on the wooden walkway, it hit. The pain in my back was sharp and I lost my breath as I fell to the ground.

CHAPTER
Nineteen

JOSEPH WAS CARRYING ME over his shoulder, running strenuously down the boardwalk. Pain shot through my body with each step he took as I was jostled about.

I could feel the veins in my face swell and pressure in my head from being upside down. Blood from the wound on my chest had soaked my shirt and was pouring down my neck onto my face, dripping onto the ground and on his legs as he ran.

Behind us, I could hear yells and the sound of footsteps chasing us. An arrow whizzed by Joseph's leg, barely missing him. Is that what had hit me, an arrow?

"Andrew," he asked with great effort, "are you awake?" I was, but I was too weak to answer, and whatever words I was trying to speak were a jumbled mess. My vision was teetering between blurry and clear, and I felt I could black out again at any moment. I hated that feeling, kind of like when you stand quickly, and everything spins and turns grey.

"Andrew!" he yelled. He was out of breath. I was surprised he was able to carry me as far as he did. He reached the railing near Eden and began pulling me over. As he did, I could see kids approaching. Their indiscernible shapes were maybe a hundred meters away.

He pulled me over his shoulder once again and began the trek over the trees and rocks. He wouldn't make it. Not with me, not with my weight on this uneven ground. If one of us were caught, it would be me. I struggled for him to let me go.

"I love you," I said to him with a voice I didn't recognize as my own. I didn't even know if he understood me.

"Andrew," he pleaded with tearful emotion.

"Go, now," I said just as another arrow hit me in the leg. I fell on my back and watched him disappear over the embankment. I lay motionless and closed my eyes.

"Is he dead?" the voice of a girl asked. I remained still and tried not to breathe, which lessened the pain from my wounds somewhat.

"I think so," said another girl. I must have been a sight if they believed me to be dead.

"Let's go after the other."

I could hear their footsteps retreat and continued holding my breath until their sounds were distant. I gasped for air and opened my eyes. And now, I needed to get up. But when I tried, I fell backwards and blacked out.

I was being carried, but not by anyone I recognized. Certainly not by Joseph. It was a boy, and he was carrying me through a field. I could see a white house in the distance through strands of yellow wheat. It was dilapidated, barely standing I would have guessed. Several kids waited in front armed with rifles. I didn't bother to struggle. I couldn't have if I tried. Even if I did escape, I would have been an easy target. I blacked out again.

I awakened on a soiled bed mattress. My chest and my leg were bandaged tightly with ripped sheets, stained with my blood. I was feverish. I could hear voices downstairs and within thirty minutes footsteps up the wooden stairs to the dark room where I lay. I contemplated closing my eyes and pretending that I was asleep, but instead I tried to sit up when a boy entered.

He had to be older than twelve, maybe thirteen, but how? The odds of surviving the virus decreased exponentially after our age. His skin was flushed red, especially in the center of his face. His hair was a dirty blonde and matted down to his head. He had blue eyes and bushy eyebrows. He was a medium build, and much heavier than me.

"You're awake."

"How long was I out for?"

"Three days."

Three days! "I need to get back to my family," I said trying to move from my position on the floor.

"You're not going anywhere," the boy responded. "How do you feel?"

"I feel weak, hot."

"It's the infection from the wounds. We tried to clean them as best we could, but we don't have antibiotics. You wouldn't happen to know where we could get some?"

I knew. Bella had amassed a substantial number of them. The fact that they had dressed my wounds meant that they had intended on keeping me alive. Maybe they were friendly. I shook my head feeling that it would be less obvious that I wasn't telling the truth.

"You said you want to go back to your family, where is that? Is it near where we found you?"

I didn't know how much this boy knew. I didn't even know how far away we were from Crawford Lake. Thoughts ran through my feverish mind, and I was exhausted. I nodded, "we were visiting the lake."

"I think you were doing more than that, you see, I think you were staying around that area."

He looked at me. I remained silent; my eyes were still heavy.

"My soldiers have been watching that area from afar, and there is another group there, trying to get into a building that is underground. Is that where you were staying?"

Soldiers he said. He referred to other kids as his 'soldiers.' Is this what the world had resorted to? Kids, shooting arrows at one another, carrying guns, and gathering into little armies. At least they were unsuccessful at getting into Eden and clearly didn't know what was in there. I was worried about Joseph. I wondered if he made it, if he were caught, I had to get back home.

"Yes," I blurted out. I looked at him in the eyes. He was not my friend. He was my enemy. He was keeping me alive because he suspected that I could give him something. I needed him to get back home.

"What's in the building?"

"Nothing, it's a tomb. It was meant to hold the bodies of the dead, but there's nothing in there." I said flatly. I felt myself getting weak.

"Sleep," he said, leaving a glass of water and a couple of pain killers on the floor in front of me. My answer had pacified him, at least for now.

I awakened again. The boy had come back and was sitting with his back against the wall in front of me. His legs were crossed. "You're still with us?" he asked.

I remained silent and took the glass of water and pain killers that were left in front of me.

"How many are there in your... family?" he asked.

"There are just a couple of us," I responded. He didn't seem to react to this, so I could tell that he didn't know.

"It's just a matter of time before the other group gets into that building. From the noises we hear. It sounds like they're trying everything."

I tried to keep my face blank, devoid of emotion. I knew the building was secure and it gave me some comfort knowing that they were still unable to get in. They clearly hadn't found the second exit.

"All that's in there is an empty space?" I could tell that he didn't believe me. I kept silent. "If you want any hope of seeing your... family again, you'd better start talking," he said before he began to stand.

"Wait," I said. I could tell that he was pleased by this. "I know of another place, another building, and it is abandoned, if I tell you where it is, will you let me go?"

He knelt in front of me. "Why didn't you take this place?"

"Because we had a place. Like I said, there's just a couple of us."

"Where is this place?" he asked.

"I will take you there, but only if you let me go."

"You can barely walk, you're feverish, and you won't make it probably more than a few days." He took a mirror off the dresser in the room and put it in front of me.

I was ghostly pale. My eyes were dark. Sweat formed on my brow and kept my hair clinging to my head. More reason, I thought, to convince him.

"I'll make it. If I die, you'll never find this other place."

He stood again. I could tell my plan was working.

"Okay, we'll leave in an hour. If you disappoint me, I'll shoot you myself."

I needed help standing and it took a few minutes for me to gain my balance. I was weak and my body felt light. They had given me something that resembled bread to eat, but it didn't sit well. When we exited the house, the light burned my eyes.

A girl and boy accompanied us and held me by either arm. Both were younger, maybe ten.

"Where is this place?" the boy asked me again.

"Which direction is the lake?" I asked him and he pointed to the west.

"That's Guelph Line," he said.

"Then we go that way," I said nodding my head to the Northeast.

We walked into the forest; it was rough going.

"How do we even know he's telling the truth?" the girl complained.

"Silence," the boy said.

I wondered how they met, how they became *his* soldiers. They weren't related. I could tell. Eventually, we hit a trail, which widened.

"It's ahead," I said, "but I need to rest for a moment." I was exhausted, and I needed some energy for what was to come. I only hoped that my plan would work. I had been running it through in my mind repeatedly. He agreed and we sat on a log at the side of the path.

The boy instructed the others to give me some water, and I drank as much as they offered. I could tell that his minions were annoyed. They whispered to each other. I was pretty sure that if it were up to them, they would have left me for dead. In some small, but peculiar way, I was grateful for this. At least I fell into the hands of someone who gave me a chance. A chance to get home. After about ten minutes, I stood up uneasily.

"Okay, I'm ready," I said, and we began to walk along the path.

When we reached the caves, I led them into the brush, to the door, to the electronic keypad.

"What is this?" the boy asked surprised. They had the same reactions that we'd had. For so long, they hadn't seen electricity. It gave them confidence, stoking their ego, and made them pay less attention to me.

"It's the other building," I said. I entered the code and the door opened.

I walked inside. "Are you coming?" I asked them. They were still bewildered and silently my three captors entered. I pressed the first floor. The lab.

As the elevator reached the first floor and the doors opened, I walked out first, making a point of clumsily brushing past the girl, which I could tell annoyed her even more.

The three of them walked out and beyond me. They were fascinated as they looked around the room. They spoke of the potential of the space. It was then, while they were captivated by the lab, that I slipped back into the elevator and pressed the close button.

One of them got off a shot. It startled me, but to my surprise the glass didn't break.

"Where's the button?" the boy yelled; his voice muffled by the glass.

I shook my head slowly.

He began to shoot the glass in rapid succession, but it didn't break. He put his hand on the handprint, but it flashed red. All sorts of obscenities came out of his mouth, and I just smirked. I pressed the ground button, and the elevator began to ascend. I had captured my captors.

The story will continue...

Devon Rhys is an alternative rock musian and author. He writes LGBTQ-positive novels for young adults. He is a three-time college graduate and lives in downtown Toronto, Ontario, Canada. His music is available on iTunes, Spotify, and other digital distribution channels. Visit Devon at devonrhys.com and follow along on Instagram and Facebook at @devonrhysmusic

www.ingramcontent.com/pod-product-compliance
Lightning Source LLC
Chambersburg PA
CBHW051226210726
48290CB00003B/824